Ella whipped around as the car gunned straight for them.

A dark shadow of a face loomed behind the tinted windshield. The killer was coming for her.

"It's him!" she yelled, reeling.

"Get back!" Roman barked, his arms coming around her and yanking her to the icy ground. And then she was rolling, cold earth seeping through thin clothes, blades of frozen grass scraping her cheeks.

Tires crunched, too close, the vehicle blasting forward and barely missing them. Roman pushed her behind him, slid his gun from its holster. Aimed.

The first shot hit a back tire. Rubber burst, debris flew. Ella scrambled backward, expecting the car to reverse, its tires to swerve toward them. Another shot split the air, the back windshield crashing in.

"Move, move, move!" Roman yelled, grabbing onto Ella's arm and pulling her farther away from the lot, ready for the driver to try to strike again...

Sara K. Parker has been a writer ever since she was gifted a 4" x 6" pin-striped journal for her tenth birthday. Her writing hobby has since grown into her dream career—writing for Love Inspired, freelancing for magazines and teaching English at a community college. She and her husband live in Northwest Houston with their four children, two (soon-to-be three!) mischievous dogs and an extremely vocal senior cat.

Books by Sara K. Parker

Love Inspired Suspense

Undercurrent
Dying to Remember

DYING TO REMEMBER

SARA K. PARKER

H **HARLEQUIN**® LOVE INSPIRED® SUSPENSE

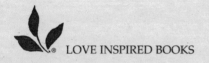

LOVE INSPIRED BOOKS

ISBN-13: 978-1-335-54377-6

Dying to Remember

Copyright © 2018 by Sara K. Parker

www.Harlequin.com

Printed in U.S.A.

It is of the Lord's mercies that we are not consumed,
because his compassions fail not. They are new
every morning: great is thy faithfulness.
                                        —Lamentations 3:22-23

To Kai, Noah, Rayne and Aaliyah—
You are my fiercest encouragers and my very own
live-in comedians. You are also kind, compassionate
and stronger than you know. Your smiles and laughter
remind me daily to lay every burden at the feet of Jesus
and seek joy. May the years ahead be full of happiness,
love, growth and opportunities to bless others.

ONE

The car was gone. Ella Camden was sure of it.

She'd spent the better part of twenty minutes peering through the taxi's back window just to be certain.

Somewhere amid Friday rush hour traffic between Route 97 and the Baltimore-Washington Parkway, the silver sedan that had been following her had disappeared.

"I don't see it anymore," she said into her cell phone, finally facing forward again and slumping against the seat.

"Don't you dare have that driver turn around," Autumn Simmons responded, her tone unusually serious.

That was exactly what Ella wanted to do, though: tell the cabdriver to forget it. Turn the car around and take her back to her mom's house. She sank down lower in her seat, her grip tight on the phone. "I'm probably just being paranoid," she said, echoing the words of her sisters, several coworkers, her doctors…everyone except Autumn. "My injury—"

"Don't even go there." Autumn cut her off. "No way you've imagined a silver car following you home three days in a row."

Her friend's words brought on an unsettling mixture of reassurance and fear. On the one hand, it was a relief to know that she had an ally who didn't think she was losing her marbles. On the other hand, Autumn's support meant that Ella could truly be in danger. If she was in danger, she needed help. There was only one place she could go for that, one person who might be able to figure things out—which was why she'd had the driver change course in the first place. But now she was having second thoughts.

"The office is probably closed," she hedged, knowing full well she could simply make a phone call to find out.

"Look," Autumn said, her voice urgent. "If you turn around, I'll take myself up there right now and tell Roman DeHart you're too chicken to face him, but you need his help."

Autumn's pushy nature was as much an annoyance as it was a confirmation that this was no time to take risks. Ella hadn't realized how much she'd missed their friendship. She'd let distance and time do what they did best—water down old memories and fill the empty spaces with new ones.

"I'm not chicken." Well, maybe a little. Though she'd never admit to it. "But what if this is all what the doctor's been warning me about? Memory lapses. Confusion. Paranoia." She touched the hat that covered her healing wound.

"Paranoia doesn't explain what happened to Marilynn. Or your mom," Autumn said.

"The police—"

Autumn cut in. "You *know* something's going on."

"That's the problem. I *don't* know… What if I'm wrong?"

"What if you're right?"

If Ella was right, then someone had tried to kill her last month and that same someone was looking for another opportunity. If she was right, her mother's accident and Marilynn Rice's death were somehow connected. After all, the two had been close friends and had worked together at Graceway, her mother's nonprofit, for years.

No question about it. If Ella was right, she needed Roman's help.

"Exactly," Autumn said as if she'd read Ella's thoughts in the empty silence. "Now, are you going to pay Roman a visit or am I?"

Ella wasn't sure if she was ready to see Roman again after all these years and she didn't like ultimatums. But she knew Autumn was right. She needed help, and Roman's security company was the best place to turn.

She sighed into the phone. "I'll do it." Ending the call, she scanned the traffic outside her cab for the sedan once more.

Her stomach churned and she pressed a hand to her abdomen. The meds made her nauseous, but she'd keep taking them for now. Intermittent nausea was better than the explosive migraines that had been plaguing her for weeks. And at least her mood had stabilized. Her doctor had pushed an increase in the dosage of her Prozac, reminding her that her memory lapses may subside when her emotions were more regulated. But while the meds had helped with her anxiety, Ella knew she wasn't depressed, and she certainly didn't need more medicine.

She needed the truth. And she needed help.

Fear crawled along the back of her neck as she peered out the back window. Still no silver sedan. She was pretty certain it was a Toyota Camry, but the car had never been close enough for her to make out the driver. Ella faced forward again, watching as Baltimore's Inner Harbor came into view, city lights glimmering against dark waters.

After-work traffic and icing roads didn't seem to faze the taxi driver as he weaved through the city. Ella wanted to tell him to slow down. Maybe just turn around all together. It was after six on a Friday evening, after all. Roman had probably left the office by now.

She half hoped he had.

More than six years had passed since they'd parted ways. Six years since his sister's murder had devastated them both and torn their relationship apart. She wondered if time had been kind to him. If he'd learned to smile again. To laugh.

If he'd gotten married, had kids.

She'd wondered for a long time, but it had been years since she'd tried to find out.

The car pulled over and slowed to a stop. She should have called, set up an appointment.

No turning back now.

Ella's gaze traveled across the sidewalk and up the grand entrance where the Shield Protection logo was boldly printed above a set of mammoth mahogany doors.

A knot of regret tightened in her stomach. Roman and his dad had purchased the historic building together, Roman's brothers joining in on the renovation in memory of their sister. Roman had sent Ella a personal invitation to the grand opening four years ago, which she had initially declined. She had started a new life for herself in Colorado, and she knew that seeing Roman again would threaten the progress she had made toward putting the past behind her.

Only, at the last minute, she'd hopped on a plane, telling herself she owed the DeHart family her support—and convincing herself that the trip would bring closure. She had never been so wrong in her life. No sooner had she stepped out of her rental car that afternoon than she'd spotted Roman hand in hand with a striking redhead. Maybe Ella shouldn't have been surprised or hurt that he had moved on, but she simply hadn't been able to face him, so she'd left the event before anyone had even realized she was there.

"You all set?" the driver asked, watching her in the rearview mirror.

"Yes, could you wait here?" she asked as she pushed the door open. "I'm not sure how long I'll be…"

He shrugged. "Meter's running."

She didn't care. It was freezing outside—unseasonably so for Maryland in November—and she didn't relish the idea of standing at the curb trying to flag down another taxi when she was ready to head back to her childhood home in Annapolis. Especially when the stranger in the silver car could reappear at any moment.

She opened the door and stepped out onto the sidewalk, taking a quick look up and down the street. She still didn't see any sign of that car. Pushing aside self-doubt, she lowered her head against the bitter wind and carefully navigated the salted but still ice-slick steps of Shield.

She grabbed hold of the wrought-iron railing with a gloved hand. Six steps up and she was standing at the doors reading the posted sign that they closed at 5:30 p.m. Disappointment warred with relief. The silver car was gone for now and at least she could truthfully tell Autumn she'd attempted to see Roman.

She pressed the doorbell anyway, just to be sure. Waited a couple of seconds and turned toward the cab. She would call in the morning to make an appointment.

She'd only taken two steps when she heard a voice as familiar as her own heartbeat.

"May I help you?"

Her heart jolted and she turned to the doors, peering up at the security camera.

"Sorry," she said. "I know you're closed…"

"Ella? Is that you?"

"Yes."

"I'm buzzing you in. Take the elevator up to the fifth floor. I'll wait for you there."

A clicking noise sounded and Ella reached for the door, pulling it open and stepping inside.

She removed her gloves and tucked them into her purse, then tugged at the edges of her cap to make sure it was secure.

A reception desk sat empty, its black granite shiny and clean. Ella's boots squeaked along the hardwood floors as she made her way to the elevator.

Inside, she pressed the number five and clenched her hands together as she ascended. Five floors were all that stood between Ella and the man she'd spent the last several years learning to live without.

Five floors and five million heartbeats.

The doors slid open and there he stood, wearing a sharp suit and a warm smile—a devastating combination that stole her breath. Ella exited the elevator, stopping just short of stepping into his arms. She shoved her hands into her coat pockets.

"Ella," he said, his voice all low and smooth like it had always been, his eyes searching hers. "It's been a long time."

She nodded. "Six years." And five months and a handful of days. He looked every bit the man she'd known—only since she'd last caught a glimpse of him he'd shaved off his goatee and bulked up at the gym.

Her gaze darted around him and down a hallway with glass doors and gleaming wood.

He touched her arm and warmth seeped through the wool of her coat.

"Are you okay?"

Ella drew a shaky breath and looked into eyes that had always been able to read her heart.

"I don't think so, Roman. I need your help."

His eyes narrowed and he gestured down the hall. "Let's go to my office."

Ella Camden was the last person Roman had expected to see when he'd heard the doorbell moments ago. A new client in need of help, maybe. Someone looking for work, likely. Ella, the woman he'd never stopped loving? Not even on his radar.

Her boots tread quietly along the hallway behind him and he opened the door to his office, letting her pass through first. She'd cut her hair. Coppery brown barely peeked out below the light gray knit cap she wore. She kept her hands in the pockets of a black winter coat and didn't meet his eyes as she entered.

"What a view," she said, moving to the floor-to-ceiling windows in his office.

The dismal gray evening had grown darker, but the harbor beyond Roman's office was lit up and bustling with Friday nightlife.

"What you've built here is amazing, Roman," Ella said, turning back toward the office and absently plucking a business card from the holder on his desk. She traced a thumb over the print, her gaze unreadable.

She seemed genuinely impressed and Roman almost asked why she'd waited so long to come see it for herself. But this meeting wasn't about them. "I had a lot of help," he said instead, waiting for her to explain why she'd come.

She was too skinny. Even with the bulky winter coat he could see that. Her eyes hadn't changed, though, their soft green-gray pulling him into memories long tucked away. And better kept there, he reminded himself. He'd spent years burying those memories under a relentless workload that didn't leave room for regret. But coming face-to-face with Ella brought it all screaming back.

"Want to have a seat?" He moved to his chair, pushing aside his closed laptop. He'd just been packing up to head home when Ella had arrived. But he wasn't in a rush. The only thing waiting for him at home was a fridge full of leftover take-out and his niece's lop-eared bunny he'd gotten stuck babysitting.

"Thanks." She took the seat opposite his, tucking his business card into her purse. "I didn't know where else to go."

Her eyes brimmed tears that she didn't let fall.

Roman's heart constricted. Years ago, he would have pulled her into his arms, but they didn't know each other anymore.

"Here." He stood and reached over to the bookcase for a box of tissues, passing them to her. "Why don't I put on a pot of coffee? We'll get you warmed up. Take your time."

She shook her head, accepting the box of tissues but not pulling one out. "No, I don't want to keep you any longer than necessary."

"We can take as long as you need."

"That's nice of you to say, but we both know it's late on a Friday and you're probably ready to get home," Ella started. "It's been all these years, and the first time I see you, I'm asking for help."

"How about you tell me what's going on and we can decide that together?"

She nodded, weariness in her expression. "I don't really know where to start, but I think I'm being followed."

"By who?"

"I wish I knew." She tugged her cap more snugly over her ears. Why didn't she take it off? She couldn't still be cold. It was a thousand degrees in the office.

Or maybe it was just him. Roman loosened his tie.

"So, you're here because you want me to find out?" he asked.

She smiled half-heartedly. "It's complicated."

Nervous. He'd never known her to be nervous. He waited.

"My mom's in the hospital," she said finally. "In a coma."

"My dad told me," Roman said. "Terrible accident. I'm so sorry, Ella. Is there any improvement?"

Ella shook her head. "That's why I came out here. I took a leave of absence from my clinic."

When she'd left to pursue veterinary school in Colorado, she'd had a singular mission: to finish school and then buy her own practice in the mountains. She'd obviously accomplished her goal. Roman had never doubted she would.

"What about your sisters? Have they been able to help, too?"

"Yes, but Bethany has three kids now, so time away is hard to come by. Holly was able to get leave for a few weeks, but she's back overseas at least until May. Even if we could all be here more often, Graceway can't function without my mom."

Two years after Ella's dad had left the picture, her mother had single-handedly opened the women's shelter. Even though she employed a substantial staff, she'd always been the one at the helm, making all the decisions.

"How long have you been out here?"

"About five weeks." She leaned forward, eyes locked on his. "But I don't remember all of it because three weeks ago, I wound up in the hospital with a...brain injury."

Roman straightened, his gaze catching on her knit cap.

"I was shot. And everyone's telling me I did it," she said, the words rushing together.

"You did what?"

"Shot myself."

"Tried to commit suicide?" The words didn't fit right in his mouth. Ella, suicidal?

She nodded.

"The thing is, I really don't think I did."

"But others think you did?" he prodded. "Who?"

"The police. The doctors. Even my family."

"You don't remember the incident?"

She shook her head. "I don't remember anything about it. I don't remember much about the weeks before, either. The doctors think my memories will come back over time."

"What did the police find?"

"From what they could figure out, I was shot—or shot myself—sitting up in bed. The trajectory was off, so the bullet only grazed the side of my head. I fell sideways and cracked my head on the edge of the nightstand before I ended up on the floor."

"The trajectory was off?" Roman asked. Possible in an attempted suicide, if she'd been waffling on her decision.

Ella shrugged. "That's what I've been told. Holly had just pulled up to the house and gotten out of her car when she heard the gunshot and came running. I was on the floor, blood everywhere."

"Even your sister thinks you were trying to kill yourself?"

Ella nodded, her lips set in a grim line. "My fingerprints were on the gun. Gunpowder on my hand."

The evidence definitely suggested a suicide attempt, but Roman didn't point out the obvious. "Do the police have any other suspects?"

Her gaze dropped to her lap. "No. They've closed the case. It happened at my mom's house.

No signs of forced entry. No signs of a struggle." She looked up at him again. "And I supposedly typed a note and left it open on my laptop before I…" Her voice trailed off.

He considered the story for a moment. No wonder the case had been closed. "If someone had tried to kill you and make it look like a suicide, he would have had to get out of the house fast since your sister showed up right as you were shot."

"My room is at the end of the hall near the garage. It's possible."

Maybe. He remembered the layout of the house, though, and it wouldn't have taken her sister more than a minute to unlock the door and run down the hall to Ella's room.

"Who would want to kill you, Ella?"

"I have no idea," she responded.

"What you're thinking happened, though… it's not a random act. There'd have to be motive. Personal motive."

He thought for a moment. After his sister Brooklyn's death, Ella had gone into a deep depression. It was no secret, as her mother had reached out to friends and the church for prayers and help.

"Could it be someone from the past? Someone who knew you had struggled with depression?" he asked.

"I really don't know, Roman," she said, frustration deepening the lines along her forehead.

"Okay." Roman softened his tone. "But if you don't remember the incident, how do you know someone else did this?"

"Because I know *I* didn't," she said simply.

Roman saw conviction in her eyes. Knew *she* believed what she was saying. But he didn't know what to make of it all.

"You don't believe me." Her words were as cold as the air outside, but she couldn't hide the hurt that flashed in her eyes.

"I do believe you." At least, he believed she was in trouble. If someone was after Ella, then Roman needed to help her. If not…if she was suffering some kind of mental illness, he still needed to help her. "Tell me more about who's following you."

She stood abruptly and Roman did, too. Her nose had pinkened, her eyes shining with unshed tears again. "Sorry. Just… I need to use the restroom." She glanced around in question.

"It's down the hall from the elevator, back the way we came."

She nodded. "I'll just be a minute."

Roman sat, drummed his fingers on his desk. Uneasy. That's how he felt. Ella was acting all wrong. He watched the clock as a full minute ticked by. Then he heard the distinct ding of the elevator.

He jumped up and ran out of his office to the reception area beyond, checking the surveillance monitors. He caught a glimpse of Ella's coat as the elevator doors slid shut behind her.

Planting his palms on the desk, he watched the downstairs lobby on the monitor. The elevator opened and Ella ran for the exit as if she was being chased. Roman frowned as he watched her hurry along slippery stairs to the sidewalk and the waiting cab at the curb. He didn't know what Ella was running from, but he wasn't about to let her run alone. He'd done that years ago and he'd never forgiven himself.

Ella's hands trembled in her lap. It had happened again. The sudden bout of confusion. One moment she was sitting across from Roman having a conversation and the next she was overcome by confusion, her mind racing with questions. *Why was she with Roman? What were they even talking about?*

Like she'd done at Graceway each day, she'd excused herself to the bathroom. There, she would calm the rising panic, try to ascertain reality, and then get back to whatever she'd been doing.

But on the way to the restroom tonight, panic had risen like a pot boiling over. She knew it was happening but couldn't head it off. She wasn't thinking about Roman or the silver car or why exactly she was running. She just ran.

Ella peered through the back window. It was

too dark to differentiate car colors. If she was being followed, she'd never know it. Her mind raced in time with her heart, her head throbbing from exertion.

She pulled Roman's business card from her purse, texting him a lame excuse and promising to call in the morning. Then she shut down the phone. He'd try to call her, and she couldn't handle that just yet.

What if she *was* going crazy?

She'd read about things like this. One day you're perfectly normal and the next you're caught up in some sort of mysterious psychosis.

But, no. The confusion had been getting better, just like the doctors said it would. As soon as the taxi had pulled away from Shield, Ella had been struck with total clarity on what she'd just run from: Roman and her plea for him to help her. In the past weeks, it had often taken her a couple of hours to regain clarity over what she'd been doing before the lapse.

The taxi slowed around the corner and pulled up in front of her mom's tired 1940s home. She'd had the Cape-Cod-style house repainted in recent years, a deep grayish blue she'd said was peaceful. Tonight, it looked dull and foreboding. Even the gentle glow of the streetlamps and porch light didn't brighten up the home. Guilt reared up as Ella paid the driver and stepped out into the frigid night. Mom's garden beds along the porch were untidy and the big maple needed a trim before a storm came and knocked it onto the house.

She fished out her keys and unlocked the front door, casting a quick glance behind her as the taxi pulled away. The street was dark and empty, no lurking silver Camry anywhere in sight. Still, fear clawed at the edge of her mind. Paranoia, she reminded herself. She stepped inside quickly, shut the door and locked up.

She set her purse on the console table near the front door, then unzipped her boots and hung her coat and hat in the tidy foyer closet. Turning on lights as she walked toward the living room, she leaned over the couch and patted Isaac's soft head.

"Hey, bud," she said to her mom's dog, sidling past the couch to grab the television remote. Isaac looked up from the living room couch, but didn't actually move a single limb in greeting. His peaceful quiet put Ella at ease, warmth rushing over her as the comforting sounds from the television filled the room. She hated the silence in the house, but as long as Isaac was content on the couch, she could be sure she was alone. He was a funny old guy, about the size of a basketball and almost as round. He was also perpetually silent, unless he met a stranger. She flipped on the news and set the remote on the coffee table. Her gaze passed over the book an acquaintance at church had brought her and she rolled her eyes.

The Prodigal Son Returns wasn't Ella's choice reading material. She figured there was a hint somewhere in the gift—a quiet reminder that Ella had been gone too long when her mom had needed her most. Shoving the guilt aside, she moved into the kitchen.

She plunked her keys down on the gray-blue Corian countertop and opened the small cabinet next to the fridge. It was packed with a hodge-podge of cooking spices, along with a stockpile of her mom's medications. Ella grabbed a bottle of aspirin, her gaze catching on the sleep meds she'd quit cold turkey as soon as she'd been re-leased from the hospital. She'd been taking the pills regularly for years, and she was convinced their effectiveness was one of the reasons she hadn't woken to the intruder the night she'd been shot. She pressed the cabinet shut, frustrated. She wouldn't get much sleep tonight. Again. But she'd rather be sleep-deprived than dead. She opened the fridge and peered inside.

She was down to the last bottle of iced tea. She'd have to hit the store tomorrow. Her hand closed around the bottle just as a swish of move-ment whispered behind her.

Ella gasped as an arm snaked around her mid-dle, dragging her back from the fridge, her feet falling out from under her. She screamed, the iced tea crashing to the floor, her hands prying at the strong arm subduing her.

A sharp sting lanced her upper arm and this time her scream was soundless as she desperately tried to twist away. She registered everything in slow motion, it seemed. A syringe in her periphery, held by a black-gloved hand. Isaac whining at her feet, his tiny claws clicking on the tiled floor as he followed the scene. Futilely, she tugged at the arm dragging her across the kitchen. But her limbs felt loose, her strength ebbing.

Her heart was beating erratically, her hands tingling and numbing, dropping away involuntarily from the arm that was holding her. She tried again to scream, but nothing happened. The house was spinning. Or was she? Nausea roiled in her gut. Panic swirled in her mind. She needed to escape.

But first, she needed to sleep.

TWO

Roman slowed as he turned into his old neighborhood. Eastport was an eclectic waterfront community with low crime. Cars lined the curbs of narrow streets where kids often played outside until after dark, though likely not tonight with this brutal cold.

Just minutes after Ella had run off, she'd texted him a vague apology, promising to call in the morning.

He didn't know what to think about Ella's story, but he knew one thing: she needed help. It was too late for her to rescind. Roman was going to help her whether she wanted him to or not. And he didn't plan to wait until she called in the morning.

After quickly locking up the building, he'd headed straight across the city, stopping only to fill his gas tank. He hoped he was right to assume Ella was staying at her mom's. He'd grown up only two blocks from the Camdens, but hadn't visited the area since his parents had moved a few years back.

Still, he easily recognized the home and parked at the curb. Stepping out into the night, he walked up the cracked driveway toward the house.

Gray-white puffs of air seeped out from underneath the garage door, a car idling inside.

Was Ella planning to head out somewhere? He stood still in the driveway for a moment, his breath swirling in the biting winter air as he waited to see whether the garage door would slide open or the car would turn off. When neither happened, he walked up the porch steps to the front door.

He knocked, noting the peeling paint and tattered silk-floral welcome sign. Looked like Julia Camden could use a little help with the old place. Maybe Roman could swing by sometime and offer a hand, fix up a few things to welcome Ella's mom home after she recovered. *If* she recovered. From what he'd heard, the prognosis wasn't good.

Roman rang the bell and knocked again, stepping back to scan the house. The shades were drawn in all the windows and, aside from the dim porch light, all was dark. A whisper of unease crept up his neck. He pounded on the door, loudly this time.

"Ella?" he called. "It's Roman."

Still nothing. He jiggled the knob. Locked.

Someone was in the garage with the car idling.

And less than an hour ago, Ella had been sitting in his office telling him everyone thought she'd tried to commit suicide…

He needed to get into the house. He ran to the garage, grabbed the latch and tried to pull the door up. Locked. He banged on it, the old metal rattling. The car kept idling, the house still and silent.

Roman raced around the side of the house and let himself into the backyard through the gate. Finding the side door to the garage, he tried the handle. It didn't budge. He yanked his wallet out of his back pocket and pried out a credit card, his hands numb from cold and moving too slowly. Pressing his shoulder against the old wood door, he worked the credit card into the groove while jiggling the knob. The lock mechanism slid free, but a dead bolt held the door in place.

The door was solid and heavy, and would take time to kick in. He'd try the back door to the house first. He darted around the corner and tried the same method there. This time the trick worked. The knob turned, the dead bolt not secured. Roman rushed into the house, flipping on lights as he went.

"Ella?" he called, moving quickly through the kitchen. His shoe crunched something on the floor, but he didn't see anything. He ran down the hall toward the garage, throwing the door open and flipping on the light.

He saw her immediately, slumped low in the front seat of a navy BMW.

No!

He ran to the driver's side, yanking the door latch—knowing it would be locked. "Ella!" he yelled, banging on the window. She was unresponsive, reclined in the driver's seat with the car still running.

They think I did it.

Did what?

Shot myself.

Roman rushed over to the toolbox and rifled around for a hammer. Grabbing it, he ran to the back-passenger door and cracked the window in one strike. Reaching through broken glass, he unlocked the car.

How long had she been in there? Even after locking up Shield and stopping for gas, he couldn't have lost more than fifteen minutes. He chanted a prayer that he wasn't too late. That, instead, he'd arrived just in time. But when he pulled the door open and reached in for Ella, she was lifeless, her eyes closed, her skin pale.

Just like he'd found his sister in her dorm room more than six years ago, murdered. But, no. Brooklyn had been cold to the touch, her skin bluish. Ella was still warm, though she didn't appear to be breathing. And lying in her open palm was a syringe.

Ella, a drug user? Roman couldn't rectify

the thought in his mind, but if she'd overdosed on something, she didn't have much time. He reached over her and shut off the car, pocketing the keys before pulling Ella easily into his arms and rushing her into the house and away from the carbon monoxide.

In the living room, he set Ella on the couch and yanked out his cell phone, dialing 9-1-1.

"Nine-one-one. Where is your emergency?"

Roman placed a hand near Ella's mouth, felt warm air. Still breathing, but too slow. He quickly rattled off the address. "I need an ambulance."

He continued to answer the woman's scripted questions even as he scanned Ella's form on the couch, looking for any other signs of injury. Nothing. His gaze caught on the right side of her head. Her hair parted unnaturally there, revealing a red scar that would take a long time to heal.

Roman sank to his knees, his hands coming up to hold hers. Had she done this to herself? He found it hard to believe, especially after what she'd told him earlier. But it had been years since he'd seen her. People changed. His heart tore at the memory of the girl he used to know. She'd been a dreamer, always looking ahead to her next goal. Always brushing off failure when it came. But then Brooklyn died, Ella's best friend since childhood and roommate in college.

At first, they had shared their grief. But one night, with one string of poorly chosen words, their relationship had shattered. He'd said things he hadn't meant. He'd been careless with his words. He'd hurt Ella, practically blaming her for his sister's death. Roman had always been ashamed, truth be told.

Ella had gone into a deep depression and the move to Colorado had seemed like her chance to break free from the darkness. What had happened to her since they'd last seen each other? Had she sunk into an even deeper depression? Started abusing drugs she would readily have available to her as a veterinarian? He turned each arm over, looking for track marks, but her skin was smooth and pale, marked only by a light spattering of freckles.

Had someone been following her as she'd suspected? Someone who wanted to make her murder look like a suicide? That seemed like a stretch. But if Ella was merely suicidal, why come to Roman for help?

The ambulance sounded in the distance and Roman unlocked the front door, leaving it open a crack. Then he remembered the syringe in the car. The doctors may need it to find out what Ella had injected herself with.

He hurried back to the garage and plucked the empty syringe from the car, then returned to the living room. A heavy sadness settled on his shoulders at the realization that the Ella he used to know might be gone forever. He crouched down again, placing a hand along her cheek. He'd missed her for years and now that she was back, she wasn't really back at all.

"You're going to be okay," he whispered. The words were both a self-assurance and a prayer. Ambulance lights blinked into the living room through the sheer curtains and voices sounded in the yard.

Someone rapped loudly at the cracked door.

"In here!" Roman called out, and the door pushed open, two uniformed medics rushing into the room.

"Found her locked in her car in the garage, engine running," Roman explained. He pointed to the syringe he'd set on the end table. "The syringe was in her hand."

The pair approached Ella quickly, one securing the syringe in a Ziploc bag while the other opened a black supply case and began an assessment. The team was efficient, and in minutes they were loading Ella onto a stretcher.

"You following us or riding with her?" one of the medics asked as they started for the front door.

"I'll be right there," Roman said. He hurried through the kitchen and locked the back door before circling back to the living room. Spotting Ella's purse, he grabbed it and then locked the front door on his way out, pocketing the keys.

The paramedics had just finished getting Ella

situated as Roman jogged up to the ambulance. He climbed in and sat alongside Ella as the siren blared and the vehicle pulled out swiftly. Slipping a hand over Ella's, Roman did the only thing he could do. He prayed.

He'd learned long ago that life was beyond his control. When his sister was killed, he'd seen the worst of humanity. He'd faced a choice then. A choice to turn away from God or to draw even closer.

Drawing closer had been the only thing that had made sense, and it was the only way he'd eventually been able to process his sister's murder to try to bring something good from it. Shield Protection couldn't ever bring Brooklyn back, but it could help keep others from meeting the same fate.

His eyes opened and settled on Ella's pale face. He prayed she'd survive tonight and that God would restore her both physically and emotionally. And he made the decision right then that he would come alongside her—something he wished he'd done years ago.

Instead grief had torn them apart and what they'd had together was long gone. But Roman could still be the friend she needed until she was healthy again.

Darkness surrounded her. Where was she? Ella took a few cautious steps, arms out in front of her. She couldn't even see her hands. No light.

Her footsteps echoed.

Or was that someone else?

She froze, holding her breath, straining to hear over the pounding of her heart.

And then, from nowhere, someone grabbed her arm.

She jerked away and opened her mouth to scream. But sound wouldn't come out. Why couldn't she run?

The hand grabbed at her arm again and she yanked away, a violent headache rearing up.

"Easy," a calm voice said. She knew that voice. She stilled.

A warm hand came to her arm, settled on it.

"Ella?"

Roman. Where was he?

"Can you open your eyes, Ella?"

Her eyes were open. Couldn't he see that? She squeezed them shut, then opened them again, her lids heavy under brash fluorescent lights.

She tried to push herself up. "Where—?"

"Shh," Roman said, his hand steady on her arm. "You're at the hospital. The nurse just needs to draw some more blood."

The hospital? Not again. Fear pierced her heart and she looked around the room.

"What happened?" she asked, her voice a broken whisper she barely recognized. She glanced down at her arm where an IV had been taped into place. The nurse began filling a vial with blood.

Roman didn't answer immediately. "Roman?"

"I came by your mom's house to check on you after you...after our meeting."

Their meeting. Right. Her skin felt hot. She'd run out on him. She'd gotten confused again. "I'm sorry, I—"

A memory flashed, a gasp escaping her lips. "Did they find him?"

Roman's expression didn't change. "Who?"

"The man who did this," she said, her voice growing stronger. "He was in the house. I was in the kitchen." The memories rushed back. "I'd opened the fridge, grabbed a bottle of iced tea, and someone was there. He attacked me. He had on black gloves and..." She reached for the memory. "He injected me with something!"

She looked down at her left arm, rotating it slightly in search of the injection site, but she didn't see any evidence of what had happened. "He dragged me down the hall. I couldn't move. I felt paralyzed." After that, she came up blank.

A slight furrow along Roman's brow showed that he'd heard. Other than that, he didn't respond.

"All done," the nurse said quietly, gathering the tubes and the rest of her supplies. "I'll let the doctor know she's awake," she added, letting herself out of the room.

Fear bubbled up in the wake of Roman's silence. "They didn't find him," Ella surmised.

Roman pulled over a chair and sat. He looked

tired, his dark hair ruffled, the buttons on his white shirt undone at the top.

"Maybe we should start from the beginning, Ell," Roman finally said.

Ella's heart skipped a beat at the old nickname, so warm in his voice a dozen memories melted out of it.

"That's all I remember from the time I got back to my mom's tonight."

"No, I mean—start from when you returned to Maryland. You came because of your mother's accident, right? Did anything seem off when you arrived?"

"I…don't know."

"You don't remember?"

She shook her head, frustrated and considering how much to reveal to Roman. Since she was asking for his help, she figured she'd be best off with full disclosure. "Since the shooting, I've had trouble with my memory," she admitted. "And my instincts."

"In what way?" Roman asked.

"It's hard to explain, but I can't trust my own mind sometimes," Ella said. "I get bouts of confusion, short-term memory loss, gaps in clarity. That's why I took a taxi to see you. I haven't been cleared to drive. The neurologist called it post-traumatic amnesia. That's what happened at your office. We were talking and then I suddenly had no idea why I was there, why I was standing face-to-face with you after all these years."

"Sounds like a scary thing to go through."

"It's unsettling."

"Is it permanent?"

"My doctor says it should get better with time. He can't predict how long the recovery will take, or whether I'll ever fully recover."

"I'm sorry, Ell."

"Don't be," she said. "I just needed you to know."

"Okay, let's explore a different question," Roman said. "If someone wanted you dead, why try to make it look like a suicide?"

She'd considered the question for weeks. "To keep the focus on me and far away from my killer?" she suggested. "If it's someone I used to know, like you mentioned, maybe he's hoping my suicide wouldn't be questioned."

"Maybe," Roman said, his dark gaze holding hers and stirring up a longing for what they used to share.

Did he believe her? She couldn't tell, but she had a feeling he wanted to.

A doctor entered the room, white coat pristine, stethoscope hanging around her neck. She smiled pleasantly and held out a hand to Ella in greeting.

"I'm Dr. Patel," she said. "How are you feel-ing?"

"Okay," Ella responded, waiting for what she

knew was to come. "Well enough to go home," she added.

Dr. Patel nodded, casting a patronizing look down at her. "We'll monitor you overnight," she said carefully. "I've ordered a psychiatric evaluation for first thing in the morning before we can clear you to go home."

"I need the police, not a psychiatrist," Ella responded.

"The police?" Dr. Patel asked.

"I didn't try to kill myself," Ella insisted, pushing herself to a sitting position. "Someone attacked me."

The doctor's mouth flattened into an expression of forced patience. "I'll arrange for an officer to meet you here," she said calmly. "But you understand, Ella, we can't just send you home without taking precautions after this second suicide attempt in as many months?"

Ella wanted to scream. Considered it. But realized that would only make her look less stable. "What I understand, Doctor, is that someone very clever has tried to kill me twice, and no one believes me."

The doctor's expression was unreadable. "You were found in your vehicle, in your mother's garage, with a rag stuffed in the muffler and a syringe in your hand," she said gently.

Well, that definitely didn't make her look any less suicidal.

"The volume of fentanyl-laced heroin you injected yourself with, plus the carbon monoxide from the car, was a potentially lethal combination," the doctor continued, pausing as if to allow Ella time to absorb the information.

Ella didn't need time; she knew exactly what fentanyl was—a powerful anesthetic when used in the medical profession and an especially dangerous street drug when combined with heroin.

"If your friend here had arrived just a few minutes later, we may not have been able to save you," Dr. Patel added.

"I need the police," Ella repeated because she could tell the doctor's opinion was set.

"I'll contact them," Dr. Patel agreed, but she didn't look happy about it. She excused herself from the room, pulling the door closed behind her.

"Roman, someone is trying to kill me," Ella said. "And I don't know how to prove it."

"Tell me exactly what you remember," he said.

She started from the moment she had arrived home earlier in the night, and told every detail she could remember up until the moment she blacked out.

When she finished, Roman looked thoughtful and a little uneasy. "You said you dropped the bottle and it shattered."

"Right. Did you see it?" she asked hopefully.

He shook his head. "I didn't, but I remember something crunching under my shoe in the kitchen. I didn't see what it was, though. I'll want to take a better look."

Hope thrummed. Maybe he'd find glass on the floor that would corroborate the story. "Does this mean you believe me?"

Roman's cell phone rang and he slid it out of his pocket. "I do," he said. "But I still need facts. I still need evidence." Then he stepped to the side to answer the phone.

From the sounds of it, Roman was making arrangements for a team member to take his place at the hospital so he could go back to her mom's place. Finally, someone besides Autumn in her corner. And not just anyone. Roman DeHart, co-founder and CEO of the most sought-after private security company in the Baltimore-Washington metropolitan area. If anyone could find proof that Ella wasn't losing her sanity, Roman was the one.

And she needed that proof quickly, before she was dead and everyone assumed she'd finally succeeded in her plan to end the life she supposedly didn't want to live.

THREE

Roman pocketed his phone and met Ella's eyes. "I've mobilized a team for your case," he told her.

"That was quick," she said. "Thank you."

"I want you to feel safe." It was quite possible that Ella was experiencing paranoia or delusions related to a mental illness, but the story she'd told him also sounded plausible. If it was correct, he wanted to get back to Julia Camden's house ASAP—before whoever had attacked Ella doubled back to clear the scene. "I'll be right outside your door until my relief gets here. Then I'll go back to your mom's and look around more thoroughly."

"My mom," Ella said suddenly. "She's here, too." She brushed off her covers. "Maybe I'll sit with her for a while and—"

"Do me a favor and wait till morning, okay?" Roman asked, cutting her off.

Ella frowned and looked like she might argue.

"It's safer to stay here, where the only people

who will have access to your room will be medical personnel or a Shield team member," he told her. "I'll take you to her personally in the morning," he assured her. "Your purse is on the countertop." He pointed across the room. "Can I grab you anything else from the house?"

She pulled the sheet back up and Roman took that as a sign of her resignation. "Could you let the dog out? I usually do one last time before I go to bed."

"I didn't notice a dog tonight…"

"Oh, no. I hope he didn't get out," Ella said.

"Don't worry—I'll find him. What's his name and what kind of dog is he?"

"He's a little Havanese mix—and his name's Isaac."

Roman grinned. "Interesting name for a dog."

"My mom always said if she'd had a son, she would have named him Isaac," Ella said with a wry smile.

Roman chuckled. "I'll find Isaac. Anything else?"

"My laptop, if you plan to swing back by here tonight. But don't make a special trip."

He didn't know what kind of work was so important she needed to get it done while sitting in a hospital bed, but he didn't say as much. By the time he would return with the laptop, she'd hopefully be asleep anyway, so he didn't argue.

Roman moved toward the door. "I'll grab the

laptop and drop it by on my way back from your mom's place. Try not to worry—you'll be out of here in no time."

He stepped into the hallway, not sure if he was right at all. Ella's story defied belief. He wasn't sure about the legalities of keeping someone like Ella hospitalized if she wanted to go home, but he'd venture a guess that any self-respecting psychiatrist who valued his medical license would probably be very nervous about sending her home tomorrow.

Clicking heels from down the hallway drew his attention and he smiled as Triss Everett came into view, long, dark hair swinging in a low ponytail as she hurried toward Roman. The rookie on the team with barely a year of experience under her belt, Triss was a force to be reckoned with. Roman had no qualms about leaving her to guard Ella for the night.

"You got here fast. I hope you weren't speeding again," he said lightly as Triss approached.

"I don't call it speeding when I'm on the job." Her face was serious, dark eyes unreadable. She was the younger sister of Roman's longtime friend Luke, but the only traits the two had in common were their dark hair and dark eyes.

"What do you call it, then?" he asked.

"Expediting my response time."

He caught the barest hint of humor in her expression and had to laugh. "You've been pulled over three times in six months," he pointed out. "I'd rather have you here a few minutes later than smashed up in a car accident."

"Noted," she responded, handing him a set of car keys. "Now, if we're done with the pep talk, I parked in the garage. Third floor, near the elevators."

The woman was always business, but that was a major asset to his team. "Let me catch you up to speed and then I'll get out of here."

Twenty minutes later, Roman stepped out of the company car Triss had driven to the hospital. The Camden home was all lit up, the lights still on from earlier in the evening. He shut the car door behind him, glancing up and down the quiet street as he tugged his gloves on. Few lights glimmered from the surrounding houses, cars dark and icing over. He pulled out his flashlight and began a slow walk around the perimeter of the home. He planned to come back in daylight, but he'd see what he could find tonight.

After circling the house and not spotting anything amiss, he let himself in through the front door. Standing in the doorway for a moment, he took stock of the living room, his gaze touching the empty, faded couch, the box television, the layer of dust over the mantel. No sign of the dog. No obvious sign that an intruder had been in the house, either. The only evidence he might be able to corroborate was Ella's story about the iced tea.

He bypassed the living room as she'd likely done, crossing the hallway and walking toward the fridge as he scanned the floor for any signs of the iced tea or the broken bottle. The floor was clean and dry, but he crouched down anyway, taking a closer look for evidence of what he'd stepped on earlier. He rubbed a hand over the glossy wood and looked at his palm. Dust particles and a few tiny flakes of what could be crushed glass.

He turned to the sink. It was empty but not dry. A damp, brown dish rag hung neatly over the faucet. He didn't pick it up, just in case the police decided to sweep through, which he thought was highly unlikely unless he could find a reason to convince them. Bending close to the rag, he could only detect the faint scent of dish soap. The trash can in the pantry was also empty, so he made a mental note to ask Ella if she had emptied it. He was almost to the hallway before he noticed a little smudge on the tile that he hadn't seen at first.

He bent closer. Darker than iced tea, redder than mud. Blood? He crouched low and looked around, saw two more prints leading to where wood met carpet. Paw prints? The dog had made himself scarce. Could he be injured?

Roman pulled out his cell phone and snapped photos of the rag and the dark smudges on the floor. That was all he could find, but it was enough to lend credence to Ella's story.

Ella said she'd dropped the tea in the struggle. That meant her attacker must have taken the time to clean up the mess to hide any signs of an attack and make it appear she'd tried to take her own life.

Resuming his search, Roman turned down the hall and entered Ella's room, which was adjacent to the garage and across the hall from the bathroom. Her room was perfectly in order, her laptop sitting closed on a small desk near the window. He picked it up and slipped it into a nearby case, then circled back to the living room still in search of the dog. He hoped Isaac hadn't gotten out during all the commotion tonight.

He looked under the couch and the mystery was solved. The old dog cowered as far back beneath the couch as possible, wide, startled eyes looking back at Roman's flashlight.

"There you are," he said, reaching under the couch.

Isaac growled a warning.

Roman figured Isaac's bite couldn't do much damage, but he assumed the poor guy felt threatened and trapped, so he lifted the end of the couch a few inches, pulling it away from the wall. The dog growled again but he didn't try to run.

Roman bent close to the little fluff ball, who

really couldn't be called "little" at all. What did they feed this guy?

"It's okay, buddy," he said in a quiet voice, moving his hand to let the dog sniff. Then he scooped the roly-poly, still growling dog into his arms.

"Hey there, Isaac," he said. "Let's see what's going on with you." He sat on the couch and turned the dog in his lap, seeing the problem immediately—a shard of glass between two of Isaac's toes. The drying blood blended with the black pads of his paw but stained the dog's white fur.

"Poor guy," Roman said, cradling the dog in his arms and standing. His mind raced. Isaac needed a vet, and Roman needed the police involved at the Camden residence. It was going to be a long night.

Ella had spent the better part of the past hour waffling between considering an escape plan and digging for memories she may have forgotten from the attack.

Since she pictured burly psych-ward security men chasing her down and wrestling her into a straitjacket, the escape plan didn't appeal. She would have to be patient and hope that the doctor tomorrow would deem her stable enough to go home.

But that left her with a lot of time on her hands.

Time to review what had happened tonight. And what had happened last month. She didn't have many clues to go by. But one thing was certain: back in Colorado, she'd been living a peaceful existence, and since her arrival in Maryland, she'd nearly died twice. And despite popular belief, the attempts on her life were not self-inflicted. Who was after her and why?

She'd done only two things regularly since her arrival: visited her mom at the hospital and worked at Graceway to try to bring the organization back to order. Her mom had fought breast cancer for almost fourteen months before being declared cancer-free in June. She'd muscled through treatments and surgeries, determined to fight hard and not miss a step at Graceway. Every time Ella had considered moving back home to help, her mother had vetoed the idea. Ella should have seen right through the act and come anyway.

While poking around her mom's office that first day back in October, it had become clear very quickly to Ella that her mother had practically been drowning under the pressure of keeping the nonprofit going.

The organization was short-staffed and underfunded. Not to mention, the finances were a mess—and an untimely computer virus had made the situation nearly impossible to sort through. Ella was itching to start looking though the files TechSavvy had recovered.

Restless, she pushed the covers off her lap and swung her legs over the side of the bed. She needed to stretch. But just as her toes grazed the cold tile, a tap sounded outside her room and the door cracked open.

A nurse Ella recognized from earlier walked in. Her short auburn hair was clipped back with several barrettes, salt-and-pepper roots belying an age she seemed determined to hide. Her name badge read Minnie, and sported a photo that must have been taken at least a decade earlier.

"How're you feeling, sweetie?" she asked, hooking up a new bag of fluids.

"Better, thanks." In truth, her head was pounding and every movement made her feel like throwing up, but she wasn't about to admit that to anyone and risk being detained longer than necessary.

"Glad to hear it," the nurse said. "Can I get you anything?"

"Water would be great."

"Of course."

"Ms. Camden?" A young woman poked her head into the room as Minnie left to fill a pitcher.

"Yes?"

The girl entered the room. She wore a long gray sweater with black leggings and heeled boots. Her straight dark hair was pulled into a neat ponytail. Who was she? And why was she in Ella's hospital room?

"I'm Triss Everett," she said pleasantly enough, but she didn't smile. "I work with Shield. Roman asked me to cover for him for the next couple of hours."

A teenager in leggings was not exactly who Ella had envisioned when Roman told her he'd set up her protection detail.

"I just came from a night class at college," Triss explained, as if reading Ella's misgivings. Then she cocked her head to the side. "Were you expecting someone else?"

"No," Ella said then shrugged. "Well, maybe," she admitted, trying to drum up energy for a conversation. "How long have you been with Shield?"

"Nearly a year," Triss said, quirking a small grin as if she knew exactly what Ella was thinking. "I may look harmless, but I'm well trained and armed. Anyway, I didn't want to disturb you if you were resting, but I peeked around Minnie when she came in, and saw you were awake."

Triss moved further into the room and perched on the edge of a nearby chair. Ella levered herself back up in bed and stuffed a pillow behind her back, the IV line pinching as she moved.

"You doing okay?" Triss asked. "Can I get you anything?"

"Unless you can get me out of here, I don't think so."

Triss looked at her seriously. "Roman would fire me on the spot."

Ella sighed, consciously slowing her breathing to try to get a wave of dizziness under control. She'd moved too fast. "I was joking."

"Maybe," Triss said, watching her observantly. "But I sense truth to it."

"I'm sure you've been filled in on the situation."

"Everyone thinks you tried to kill yourself, but you say someone is setting it up to make your death look like a suicide."

"That's it in a nutshell."

"And you want to leave the hospital because…"

"Because no one believes me, and I'm not going to find any answers trapped in this hospital bed."

Triss nodded but didn't look all that sympathetic.

"Well, I can't help you get out of here, but if you think of anything else, I'll be just outside." She pushed up from the chair and walked to the door. "Just shout if you need me. I'll check back in a bit."

"Thank you," Ella said belatedly as Triss closed the door, throwing the room into silence once again. Her gaze darted around the sterile space, her mind racing.

If she let her eyes close, she knew she'd see a gloved hand snaking around her face, glass shattering at her feet. For weeks now she'd been fitfully waking to the feel of the barrel of a gun at her temple or the echoing blast of a gunshot. Were they actually memories or was her mind simply filling in the blank spots? It was impossible to differentiate, especially because other memories had found their way into those nighttime terrors, too—memories she'd spent years mastering how to escape.

She squeezed her eyes shut against the images flashing through her mind. Memories of devastating loss and the unrelenting guilt that had been tormenting her for the past six years. An Ambien would be helpful right about now. The hospital would be a safe place to take one, and Ella would do just about anything for a few solid hours of sleep. She knew the pills had become a crutch. Her doctor had begun to advise she start weaning off of her sleep meds. But after years of counseling, kickboxing and prayer that seemed to do nothing but float hopelessly into the atmosphere, the pills had given her the first reprieve. During the days, she busied herself at work, distracted by clients and responsibilities. She kept her social calendar full and committed to a steady workout routine. All of these things she did to avoid the memory of finding her best friend—Roman's sister—murdered.

Then the night would come. And, in the dark solitude of her bedroom, memories assaulted her, relentless. The sleeping pills muted the night-mares, offering the restful sleep Ella was desperate for.

She considered asking a nurse for something to help her sleep, but she didn't want to give the psychiatrist further reason to detain her. Still, memories flooded her mind, an all too familiar sensation of panic rising.

Futilely, she took a slow, deep breath and let it release. Usually her heartbeat would slow, her calm return, but tonight Ella could not settle. No amount of counselor-advised deep breathing exercises could combat her creeping anxiety. "God, I need…" she whispered, but words failed her. What did she need? And did it even matter? It seemed to her that God had already declared the matters of life, and no amount of prayer could change His mind or His plans.

Hours later Ella woke to lights being flipped on and a nurse telling her that her psychiatry appointment would be at eight thirty. A bag next to her bed held her laptop and a change of clothes. Roman must have come by in the night and decided to let her sleep. The thought warmed her as she dressed, and somehow she felt hopeful as Triss and a nurse escorted her to her appointment.

It wasn't long before that hope turned to worry. Sitting across from Dr. Paul McClintock, his gigantic, framed degrees decorating the gray wall behind him, Ella felt decidedly like throwing up.

She wasn't sure what to expect as the psychiatrist finished typing notes into his computer. His opinion was all that stood between her going home or into a psychiatric ward. Yet, for the past hour, she'd answered question after question and stared back into his eerily calm face and expressionless eyes and had no idea what he was thinking in his highly educated mind. That worried her. Her own story worried her—it wasn't believable and she knew it.

Finally, Dr. McClintock stopped typing, looked up at her and smiled. No, he grimaced. It was definitely more grimace than smile.

"I would like to admit you for further monitoring…" he started, and Ella's hackles rose. But before she could get out a word, Dr. McClintock continued. "What concerns me the most is—"

A knock sounded at the door and the doctor looked up. "Yes?"

The door opened and Ella turned to see Roman standing shoulder-to-shoulder with a stranger—presumably a doctor, judging from his smart business attire and the stethoscope at his neck.

Roman nodded toward her, his face serious.

"I'm sorry to interrupt," the doctor said and then turned his attention to Ella. "I'm Dr. Thornton, the attending physician this weekend." He gestured to Roman. "Your friend was busy last night, working with the police on your behalf. It seems there may be enough evidence at your mother's home to suggest proof of an attacker."

Ella glanced at Roman. He looked tired, wearing the same white shirt as last night, but more wrinkled and worn, his hair a bit mussed, a shadow of stubble along his jawline.

Most importantly, he was no longer looking at her the same way everyone else had been for weeks. Somewhere in between her falling asleep and her waking up, it appeared that Roman had found a solid reason to believe in her.

"The police have been in your mom's house and have dusted for prints and taken photos." Roman filled her in. "They'd like me to take you to the station to give a statement after you're discharged."

"I've already put your discharge orders in," Dr. Thornton said.

Ella started to stand.

"Now, hold on just a minute," Dr. McClintock interjected, rising to his full height of at least six-foot-two. "How can we possibly be certain—"

"Unfortunately," Dr. Thornton interrupted firmly, "unless you discovered something alarming during this interview, she's legally free to go."

Neither doctor looked convinced, but McClintock quickly moved to his desk, sharply grabbed up his papers and turned to thrust them back into the file drawer behind him, not saying another word.

"Your nurse will get you squared away back in your room when you go to collect your things," Dr. Thornton said, brushing past Roman into the hallway. "Take care," he added as he headed down the hall, his black dress shoes squeaking along the tiled floor.

Ella fell into step beside Roman as they left the psychiatrist's office and turned toward the elevators.

"Doing okay?" he asked, his gaze sweeping over her.

"Now that I get to leave, yes," she said, her heart skipping as his palm came to her back. "What did you find at the house?"

"Let's get you out of here and we'll discuss it in the car." He jabbed the call button for the elevator.

"When do we have to be at the police station?"

"We're supposed to go directly there," Roman answered. "But we have time to visit your mom."

She was relieved he'd remembered. She tried to visit every day, hoping her mom would hear her voice and be reminded that the people she loved needed her to come back to them. But with each day that passed, Ella's hope had begun to dwindle. Years ago she'd learned that some prayer requests went unanswered, and she was afraid this may be one of those times.

Which reminded her...

"This is probably not the best time to tell you I'm supposed to be at a funeral at eleven thirty."

Roman glanced at her as the elevator doors slid open. He didn't look happy with her announcement. "Whose?"

"Marilynn Rice. She used to work at Graceway." Her throat felt tight as she stepped into the elevator. "She and my mom were really close. Her house was robbed Monday evening. It looks like she was pushed down the stairs. Broke her neck. No one knew until the next morning when she didn't show up for work."

"Ella."

She looked up at Roman as the elevator rose. "Yes?"

"Have you made the police aware of the possible connection between your mom, Marilynn and what you're going through?"

"I've tried to," she said. "But I'm not exactly what they'd call a competent or reliable witness."

The doors slid open and they stepped out into a bustling hallway on her mom's floor.

"Let's table this conversation until we get out of here," Roman said.

A half hour later, the dark clouds of a brutal winter day loomed through the glass doors ahead as Ella walked with Roman in a slight haze toward the exit. She'd had to rush the visit with her mom, but at least she'd been able to see her.

Her throat ached from held-back tears. With each passing day it seemed less and less likely her mother would ever wake up. And if she did, there was no guarantee she would be the same.

Roman pressed the door open and a blast of cold air stole Ella's breath. He draped his jacket over her shoulders and set a protective arm at her back.

She couldn't help but glance behind her at the hospital as they left. What she was looking for, she couldn't be sure. But at the edge of her memory, she was fairly certain she knew something. Something that could put an end to the questions keeping her up at night—and maybe something that could save her life.

"You're shivering," Roman said. "The car's just over—"

A screech of tires cut him off and Ella whipped around, registering the car as it fishtailed around the corner, just yards away.

"Watch out!" Roman yelled, grabbing her by the arm and yanking her off the blacktop and onto the ice-covered grass.

But the car kept coming, its engine gunning straight for her.

FOUR

"It's him!" Ella yelled, reeling back, eyes trained on the silver car.

Brakes squealed, the car turning sharply. A dark shadow of a face loomed behind the tinted windshield. He was coming for her.

"Get back!" Roman barked, his arms coming around her and yanking her to the icy ground. And then she was rolling, cold earth seeping through thin clothes, blades of frozen grass scraping her cheeks.

Tires crunched, too close, the vehicle blasting forward and barely missing them.

Roman pushed her behind him, slid his gun from its holster. Aimed.

The first shot hit a back tire. Rubber burst, debris flying. Ella scrambled backward, expecting the car to reverse, its tires to swerve toward them. Another shot split the air, the back windshield crashing in.

"Move, move, move!" Roman yelled, grabbing her arm and pulling her further from the lot, ready for the driver to try to strike again.

Instead the car jarred off the median to the parking lot, sparks flying from the wobbling tire rim as the vehicle turned sharply out of the lot.

Ella memorized the car, noting the missing license plate, the low spoiler with a white scrape on the rear left. He was getting away, but he wouldn't get far. And this time she'd have something to tell the police.

Roman was already on it, his phone to his ear as he grabbed her hand and led her deeper into the lot and toward a black SUV. She ran alongside him, only half hearing what he relayed to the police as he opened the passenger door and helped her into the car. She kept her attention fixed behind them, on the lookout for her attacker.

Roman slid into the driver's seat and started up the car, tossing his phone in the console.

"Are you going after him?" Ella asked.

"Not with you in the car," Roman responded. "He won't get very far," he added, peeling out of the parking lot. Sirens sounded nearby.

The police would track him down, Ella told herself. It'd be impossible to keep driving on that rim. She shivered, watchful of surrounding traffic as Roman pulled onto the highway.

"Does that look like the sedan you saw yesterday?" Roman asked.

"Exactly."

"It's been following you for a few days?"

"Since Wednesday after work. I caught a glimpse of the car pulling away from the curb as my taxi drove past. Something about how quickly he peeled out made me look twice. I had my driver stop at two stores and each time we pulled back onto the road, the car wasn't far behind. That's how I realized he was following me."

"You never reported it?" Roman asked, his eyes fixed on the road ahead.

"I did. Twice," Ella answered. "But I couldn't read the license plate and by the time the police caught up with me each time, the car had turned off the road."

"If this is the same guy who was in your mom's house, then he's diverging from his usual tactics. I mean, if he's trying to make it look like you're suicidal, running you over wouldn't exactly help his cause."

Ella knew Roman was right. Was the attacker getting desperate? Making mistakes? "Unless he planned to make it look like an accident," she suggested. "You know, like a drunk hit-and-run that people may be convinced was completely random. But you threw a wrench in his plans when you disabled the car."

"It's a possibility," Roman said, but Ella didn't think he held much stock in the idea. She turned in her seat and watched the highway through the back window for a moment.

"You don't have to worry about him following us out here," Roman said. "That car wouldn't make it a half mile on the highway."

Ella faced forward again, leaning her head back against the seat. "You're right. I'm just jittery."

"That was a close call," Roman said. "We'll need to work up a list of everyone you've come in contact with since you arrived in Maryland."

He glanced at her then, his expression thoughtful. "You mentioned Marilynn's death. And, also, your mom's office being in a state of disaster and some potential financial discrepancies. Is there anything else you're leaving out of the equation?"

"I feel like there's more," she admitted. "Some things I can't remember."

"From before you were shot?" Roman asked.

She nodded. "It's hard to explain, but at the edge of my mind, I think I know something that might help."

"Give it a little more time, I'm sure it'll come to you," Roman said, but the words didn't do much to reassure her.

"I hope so," she said. "One thing I keep fixating on is that two days before I came back to the office after being hospitalized, the network at Graceway got hit with a nasty computer virus."

Roman's gaze cut sharply to her. "What was the damage?"

"It wiped out a bunch of our computers," she

said. "Not even Autumn could fix the mess and she's a whiz at computers. Remember her?"

"Autumn Simmons—sure do," he said. "She works for Graceway?"

"Part-time. She's in IT. But even she couldn't recover the files. I ended up hiring a private company to the tune of a small fortune."

"Were they able to do it?" Roman asked.

She nodded, unzipping her purse. "They estimated they were able to retrieve about sixty percent of the lost files. I haven't had time to go through them, but I've got it all on this flash drive and—"

Her heart dipped as she reached into the inner zippered pocket of the purse and found it empty. "Oh, no."

"What is it?" Roman asked.

She unzipped the two other pockets of the purse, rooting around frantically for what she knew she wouldn't find.

"It's gone," she said. "I put it in my purse yesterday, zipped it into the inside pocket so I wouldn't lose it."

"Are you sure?" he asked. "You mentioned your memory—"

"I'm sure," she said, heart racing. "Whoever attacked me last night must have taken it."

"Who knew you had it?" Roman asked.

"No one." She sifted through her purse, second-guessing herself. "Maybe I never put it in my purse. Everything else is here—why would someone steal the flash drive? There was no way of knowing what was on it."

"Maybe we can swing by Graceway later and look around for it," Roman suggested.

"Good idea."

"In the meantime, I'll get you to that funeral. Afterward, we're going straight to the station and making sure the dots are being connected. I've got a friend there—Tyler Goodson. I'll call ahead."

"Thank you," she said, feeling relieved that he had a plan and that he seemed vested in her situation. For the first time in weeks, she didn't feel so alone. "What did you find last night?" she asked.

He caught her up and told her what had happened to Isaac.

"Poor guy. Is he okay?"

Roman nodded. "I got the piece of glass out, but took him to the emergency clinic anyway, to make sure I got it all. They bandaged him up."

"Thank you so much. Just let me know what I owe you."

"Don't worry about it."

They stopped at a red light just outside her mom's neighborhood.

"Unfortunately, the police don't have much to go on yet," Roman continued. "They checked all the locks at the house, but didn't find evidence of tampering. Dusted for prints. No signs of forced entry."

"I have a feeling a lot of people have had access to my mom's house in the past year or so," she said. "I know she had neighbors and employees coming in to help with Isaac whenever she was stuck at the hospital for chemo treatments. Knowing my mom, she's probably given out a bunch of keys, and who knows where they've circulated." She sighed. "What a mess."

"We'll figure it out," Roman said, his eyes dark and determined. He held her gaze for a long moment and something crackled between them, memories of long ago when they were just two teenagers in love, with a world of dreams in front of them. He reached out a hand and brushed her cheek with his knuckles.

"You're not in this alone anymore."

Her eyes stung at the tender gesture. She wanted to turn away from it, from him, from that mysterious sense of longing she felt when she looked into his eyes. But she also wanted to capture the moment.

The light turned green and Roman's hand dropped away, but his warmth was imprinted on her skin. Ella stared out the passenger window. The last thing she needed right now was a reminder of the chemistry they'd always shared. As time had worn on, she'd convinced herself she'd built the relationship up in her head, and that the feelings she remembered were par for the course when reminiscing over a first love.

Never mind that, since Roman, she'd never been on more than three dates with any man. She had been telling herself that eventually she would meet the right guy at the right time and everything would fall into place. But now she couldn't help but wonder all over again if Roman had been the one and she had lost him to one life-altering moment of selfishness.

"For now, the best I can do is offer you protection," Roman was saying, and Ella forced her mind away from pointless thoughts.

"That's all I'm asking. Tell me how it works. I'm willing to pay for the highest level of security. I've been living in fear for weeks."

"You'll have 'round-the-clock protection. Two guards at all times when you're at the house. More whenever you leave, or as the situation dictates. I'm outfitting your mom's house with a new security system and cameras. If this guy tries anything again, we'll catch him. Sound good?"

"Sounds perfect," Ella responded. She didn't deserve his help, but she needed it. Time and distance and heartache had fractured the relationship they'd shared but had done nothing to diminish her trust in him.

Roman slowed the car as he turned onto Julia Camden's street. He hadn't seen any signs of the silver car since they'd left, but he stayed vigilant as he pulled up to the home and cut the engine, his gaze roving the property. His team would arrive this afternoon to get started on the security system.

"Looks like your mom could use a little help with the old place," he said, stepping out of the SUV as Ella came around from the passenger's side.

"Yes. I should have—" Her voice broke off and Roman followed the direction of her attention. Someone was stepping out the front door and onto the porch.

Autumn Simmons. He remembered her well. A down-home country girl at heart, she'd never quite fit in with city living. But she'd always had a blast trying—the life of every party with her rich accent and bold laughter. She hadn't run in the same circles as Roman's sister, but Ella had befriended her when she'd transferred from Texas to their school during sophomore year. They'd been close.

"Autumn!" Ella said, a smile spreading over her face.

Autumn swept down from the porch, heeled cowgirl boots crunching along the yard, long, wavy hair matching her name with several shades of brown and copper.

"I've tried calling you all morning, and I've been over here three times looking for you. I was getting ready to call the police. Where on earth have you been?"

"It's a long story," Ella murmured, digging her phone out of her purse. "I guess I never turned it back on last night."

"Way to give me a heart attack," Autumn said, and then stepped back, a curious sparkle lighting her eyes. "Roman DeHart, fancy meetin' *you* here." Her Southern drawl hadn't toned down even a notch.

He offered a hand. "Autumn, it's been a long time. Nice to see you again."

She quirked an eyebrow. "It *has* been a long time." She glanced almost conspiratorially at Ella. "Five years?"

"About that," Ella said.

"Six," Roman corrected, even though it didn't matter. It had been too long. Ella had chosen to stay away, but he could have made an effort to keep in touch. It had been too painful at first and then it had just seemed...too late.

"So, what's the plan, cowboy?" Autumn asked.

Ella snorted, leading the way to the house. "He's a bodyguard, Autumn, not a cowboy. And I think the plan is to keep security around me at all times."

"You're going with her to Ethiopia, then?" Autumn asked pointedly as she followed them into the house.

"She hasn't told me about a trip to Ethiopia," he answered, his attention cutting to Ella.

"I booked a flight a few weeks ago—before I wound up in the hospital," she explained. "I rescheduled for this coming Monday."

"Why Ethiopia?" Roman was already forming his arguments against her trip, but he was curious about the destination.

"Graceway has a sister program there," Ella responded.

When she didn't elaborate, Roman knew there was something she wasn't telling him. "Okay... but that doesn't explain why you have to go there."

She sighed, kicking off her boots and avoiding eye contact. "To be honest, I don't really remember why I made the reservation in the first place," she admitted. "But there must have been a compelling reason. Hopefully it'll come to me when I get there."

"And if it doesn't?" he asked.

"Then at least I'll have a chance to check in with program staff overseas."

Her plan sounded like a logistical nightmare to Roman. "We'll talk about it later," he said, knowing they didn't have time to argue about it right now. "But if I get my way," he added, addressing Autumn, "she'll be staying in this house 24/7 until we catch this guy."

"Good," Autumn said with satisfaction, following Ella into the living room.

Apparently, Ella had one believer besides him. A believer with a key to her mom's house.

"Now, I'm ready for the long story," Autumn said, "but not too long, because I need to grab a shower and get ready for the funeral." She settled next to Isaac on the couch. Disgruntled, the dog let out a low growl and shifted his position, his tiny bandaged paw peeking out from under him.

"Bless his heart," Autumn said, tenderly patting the dog's head. "What happened to Isaac?"

"It's part of the long story," Ella said. She crouched down and inspected the bandage on Isaac's paw. "How ya doing, buddy?"

"While you catch Autumn up, I'll work on security detail for the funeral," Roman said. "Do you have the location?"

Ella reached for her purse, but Autumn was already reading the address off her phone.

"Thanks." Roman moved into the kitchen and started on his phone calls. Judging by the reckless attempt at a hit-and-run today, Ella's attacker was feeling desperate. That worried Roman most of all. Desperate people were unpredictable. He needed to get the police involved quickly, before another murder attempt could meet with success.

Marilynn Rice had lived and died alone in a sprawling bungalow overlooking the Magothy River. A chilly mist hovered over the water, adding to Roman's sense of foreboding.

Ella had offered Graceway for the wake and the church had offered its reception hall. Marilynn's sister Louise, however, had insisted on hosting the gathering at Marilynn's home—the place where she would want to be remembered.

The funeral had been tough. The burial, tougher.

When Roman was little, he'd been fascinated by cemeteries, reading the gravestones, wondering about the lives and interesting epitaphs of the long buried. But ever since Brooklyn had died, he'd done everything he could to avoid walking among gravestones. Twice a year—once on Brooklyn's birthday and once on the date of her death—he'd go to her grave. Now he stood looking down at Marilynn Rice's casket nestled between walls of cold, moist dirt. He'd never met the woman, but from what Ella had told him, she'd been a giver. A widow with no children, she'd enjoyed traveling and also working with Ella's mom, one of her closest friends.

When her neurosurgeon husband had passed away three years ago, he'd left Marilynn plenty of money and the already paid-off home. According to Ella, Marilynn had increased her hours at Graceway out of passion, not need. She'd worked faithfully for Julia Camden for years, giving her time and donating her salary right back into the organization.

Her expensive security system had caught im-

ages of her killer as he'd approached the house,
covered head-to-toe in black. Where he'd come
from remained a mystery. Police theorized an ac-
complice had dropped him off up the road, out
of view of the cameras.

Marilynn hadn't set the alarm. Never did during the day, apparently. That's how safe she'd felt
in her home of twenty-three years. Normally she
would have been at work already, but she'd taken
the day off for a couple of routine doctors' ap-
pointments.

If the intruder had arrived even ten minutes
later, Marilynn may have already left the house.
But he'd arrived at 9:50 a.m. and within twenty
minutes, Marilynn was dead and thousands of
dollars' worth of fine jewelry, along with the late
Mr. Rice's car, were missing.

Roman scanned the growing gathering of
people in the house, many of whom worked at
Graceway, according to Ella, along with several
relatives from out of state.

Mrs. Wright, the pastor's wife, was in the
kitchen with a few other ladies from church, setting out hors d'oeuvres and beverages. Classical
music played softly in the background.

To secure the home for the funeral, Roman had
posted security details at all three entrances, plus
two patrolling the grounds and one more inside
with him. Confident in his team's competence,
Roman focused on Ella as she shrugged out of

her coat and set it on a wing-backed chair in the living room. For just a moment, she paused, as if gathering her thoughts, her gaze traveling the room.

Roman's chest constricted at the sight of her standing there, fragile in a way he'd never known her to be.

Loopy silver earrings dressed up the black blouse she'd paired with a soft gray skirt. She still had killer legs. Which he shouldn't be noticing.

He crossed the room and stood next to her. "I'd like you to introduce me to the people you know here," he said, trying also not to notice the sweet scent of her hair. But a memory assaulted him…

A bonfire on a cool, late-spring night. Her after-prom party. The glow of the fire had turned her hair from copper to gold, its scent enveloping him as their lips met in the first tentative beginnings of a new relationship—

The sound of clinking glass drew his attention back to the reception as the guests turned toward the kitchen.

Mrs. Wright stood behind the granite island with a crystal glass and a spoon, a soft and sad smile on her face. "On behalf of Louise Neff, Marilynn's sister, I'd like to welcome you all to Marilynn's home."

Mrs. Wright continued with welcoming words and a prayer, followed by instructions on how to enter the buffet line set up in the adjoining formal dining room. But Roman's attention was diverted by a gentleman who stood just inside the kitchen door, his face pale and shoulders stooped. His smartly tailored suit made him appear younger than the lines on his face suggested.

As the guests started to file into the dining room, Roman leaned toward Ella. "Do you know that guy?" he asked.

"Jerry Tanner, goes by JT. He's our residential program director."

"How long has he worked for Graceway?"

"Oh, I don't know. At least five years, probably more. He and Marilynn were close friends. I'll introduce you."

She led the way across the kitchen. JT didn't look interested in getting anything to eat. He hadn't moved an inch as the rest of the guests herded into the dining room.

"Hi, JT," Ella said, offering a hand in a comforting squeeze. "I wanted you to meet my friend, Roman DeHart."

The man shook Roman's hand, sparing him a brief glance. "Good to meet you," he said. "Don't think I'll be much in the way of company."

"How are you holding up?" Ella asked.

"I'm not," JT said, his eyes glossy, and Roman was struck by the grief he saw there. "This wall is about the only thing holding me up right now."

Ella pulled a kitchen chair toward him. "Here, why don't you sit for a minute?"

"Yes, JT," Mrs. Wright said, crossing the kitchen. "Can I get you a plate? Or some punch?"

He started to sit, but froze, his eyes stricken.

"JT?" Ella said. "Are you okay?"

Roman moved in closer. The guy looked like he might pass out cold.

"Your necklace," JT said to Mrs. Wright.

Her smile fell a little and she grasped the dangling heart charm in her hand. "Hank bought it for me. Just celebrated thirty years."

JT backed away from the group. "Marilynn had a necklace just like it."

Mrs. Wright tucked the charm under her blouse. "I'm so sorry," she said. "I know every little thing can be a painful reminder."

"I think I'll just get a little fresh air," JT said abruptly, waving away the chair.

When the door closed behind him, Roman followed Ella and Mrs. Wright into the dining room, texting the property patrols to look out for JT.

"Just how close were those two?" he whispered to Ella.

"I really don't know," she said. "I'm thinking a lot closer than anyone realized."

FIVE

Ella grabbed a plate and offered it to Roman as they entered the buffet line.

"No thanks," he said. "I'll eat later." He searched the faces of the two dozen or so people in the grand dining room. The people closest to the victim—always the first place to look for suspects.

Conversation was quiet as guests filled their plates and filtered out of the room to find places to sit and talk.

Mrs. Wright smiled as they neared her. "How are you, Ella?" she asked, her tone gentle. She looked young for her age, shoulder-length blond hair stylishly cut, soft makeup and a simple black dress.

"I'm doing fine," Ella said. "Thank you." She gestured to Roman. "This is my friend Roman DeHart. Roman, this is Mrs. Wright—"

"Oh, please," the woman said with a laugh.

"Just call me Patty. You know I've told you that a thousand times, Ella."

Ella grinned. "Old habits die hard," she said with a shrug.

"Glad to meet you," Roman said, accepting the offered cups of water. "The service was beautiful. Your husband did a great job."

"I'll pass that along to him. Funerals are so hard."

"Thanks for all you did to bring this together," Ella said.

Patty's smile fell, sympathy in her expression. "I'm honored to do it. I know she and your mom were close. How's Julia? Any progress?"

"Not yet."

"I'm praying for her. The whole church is."

More guests were filtering into the buffet line behind Roman, so they excused themselves.

Ella led the way toward a small group congregated by the bay window. The pastor stood to greet them.

"Ella," Hank said. "You're looking well."

"Thank you. This is my friend Roman."

"Welcome, Roman, a pleasure to meet you." Hank extended a hand. He wore a crisp black suit with a dark gray tie, polished dress shoes and a gold watch.

At the funeral, Roman had recognized the pastor from area billboards. Anchor of Hope Fellowship had expanded over the past few years and had morphed into a mega church that rivaled those normally seen only in the Bible Belt.

"And this is Doug," Ella continued, gesturing to the young man who had appeared at the pastor's side. "Pastor Wright's son," she clarified.

His fitted suit and slicked-back hair were a bit much for the occasion, but the kind smile he directed at Ella seemed genuine.

"How's your mother?" Doug asked.

"Not much change," Ella said.

"I'm sorry to hear that." For a moment his attention strayed and Roman followed his gaze to an approaching woman with honey-colored hair and a shy smile. Doug glanced back at Ella. "We're praying for you both," he added.

"Thank you, we—"

"Lacey!" Doug interrupted her, greeting the woman with honey hair. "It's good to see you surfacing from the books. Ready for exams?"

"Still have a couple weeks to go, so not yet," the woman responded, glancing around at the group. "I'm Lacey Sage," she said with a small wave of greeting toward Ella and Roman.

"Church secretary extraordinaire," Doug added with an appreciative grin. "Too bad she's ditching us in a month. Hawaii's calling her name."

"Vacation?" Roman asked.

"Marriage," she said. "My fiancé's in the army and he's being transferred to Hawaii. I'll get a little vacation time in before starting school back up."

"What are you studying?" Ella asked.

"Business admin," Lacey said. "Just have the spring semester to go and I'll be done."

"I've tried to convince her to finish out the year here, but she's bent on that wedding," Pastor Wright teased. "Where's Gavin today?"

"He's helping his dad with a project," Lacey said. "How are the book sales?"

Doug laughed. "They've barely hit the shelves. Time will tell," he said with a shrug.

"You're a writer?" Roman asked.

"He and his dad, both," Lacey answered for both of them. "Their books came out on the same day earlier this week. *Grace for the Wayward Child* and *The Prodigal Son Returns*."

"Someone gave me your book last week!" Ella said to Doug. "I didn't notice you were the author."

"You wouldn't have—I used a pseudonym," he said. "Blake D. Wyatt."

"That would explain it," Ella said. "Congratulations to both of you—that's a huge accomplishment."

They were a warm bunch of people, Roman concluded as he listened in on the conversations. Not that he'd expected a killer to make himself known. But he'd hoped for some clues, some red flags. JT stood out, but that was about it.

As conversation flowed freely, Roman figured they'd be sticking around for a while, but it wasn't long before he noticed the droop of Ella's shoulders and the drawn look in her eyes. "You ready to head out?" he asked, and she nodded. Good, because the sooner he had her back at her mom's house in a controlled and secure environment, the happier he would be.

"Are you okay to stop by the station, or should we postpone until this evening?"

"I'll be fine," she said.

Bryan Garza, one of Shield's veteran employees, already had the SUV warming up for them when they stepped outside. "JT left a half hour ago," he reported, passing Roman the keys. "Just sat on that bench over there staring at the river and then got in his car and drove away," he added.

"Thanks for keeping an eye out," Roman said, opening the door for Ella. "We're headed to the station. Notify the crew at Julia's house we'll be back in an hour or so."

"Will do." Bryan waved and returned to his own car as Roman shut the door for Ella and went around to the driver's side.

"This shouldn't take too long," he said as he pulled away from the house. "Tyler's expecting us. I know you're tired."

"I am, but this really can't wait any longer," she said, taking out her phone and scrolling through messages.

"Agreed."

Roman pulled away from Marilynn Rice's home and drove up the winding path away from the quaint little riverside community. It was a far cry from his condo on Charles Street in Mount Vernon. He'd bought the place a few years back. It was close to work and the epitome of city living with countless options for dining and entertainment, according to his real estate agent. Turned out, he didn't have much time or inclination to take part in the social scene. He took in the pretty homes along the river, the mature trees lending shade and an element of quiet that appealed to him in a way it never had before. If he had someone to share it with, a move here would make sense.

"It's gorgeous out here," Ella remarked.

He glanced her way, reading the longing in her eyes as she watched the passing landscape. "What's it like in Colorado?" he asked.

"There are places like this out there," she said. "But I live close to my job in the city—better for business. I like it, though, and—"

Roman's cell rang, Tyler's name popping up on the caller ID on the dash. "Hold on," he said, and accepted the call.

"Roman, it's Tyler." The connection was spotty and Roman turned the speaker volume up. "We'll have to postpone the meeting," Tyler continued. "We've located the car."

"And the perp?" Roman asked.

"Gone. The car's three blocks from the hospital. Abandoned," Tyler said. "We'll run forensics on it, but we do know one thing—the car belonged to Gregory Rice, Marilynn Rice's deceased husband."

Ella's hand came to her mouth in surprise.

"I may be a while," the officer continued. "I'll stop by after we get things squared away."

"Sounds good. I'll forward you the address," Roman answered. He disconnected the call and shook his head. "Looks like our suspicions are well founded," he said.

"Whoever's after me…" Ella started to say, her face unusually pale, her words hanging in the air.

"Is also Marilynn's murderer." Roman filled the words in, just in case she was tempted to rationalize away the obvious.

"And we're only connected through Graceway," she said. "And my mom."

"Maybe before we meet with Tyler later, you can pull together a list of current and former Graceway employees going back about three years," Roman suggested. "And anyone else who had access to the building who may have had dealings with your mom and Marilynn."

"I'll see what I can do, but it'll be impossible to gather every name," she said. "My mom has a bad habit of giving the lock code out to just about anyone in need."

"It's a keyless entry?" he asked, hoping he'd heard wrong. A keyless entry was a security nightmare.

"There's a dead bolt, but hardly anyone locks it. I always do. But Mom apparently likes to keep it available for people in need."

"Why would anyone need to get in when the building's empty?"

"Autumn said Mom was forever giving the code out to people who called after hours. She'd give the code so they could have shelter, and she'd meet them at the office."

"Isn't there a residential center? Why meet them at the office?"

"The residential center is always on a waitlist. My mom would meet people at the office for emergencies. She'd help pay a utility bill or rent, or get them transportation to a local shelter."

"Not good," Roman said under his breath.

"I know," she agreed. "But I'll see what I can come up with. There's a visitor log at the office. Any name logged in after-hours probably had the lock code."

"Well, that's a start. You should probably also try to come up with a list of everyone who had access to the house."

"I'll have to call my sisters. Maybe talk to the neighbors." She sighed, leaning back against her seat.

"You look like you may need to get a little rest before making a bunch of phone calls," Roman said.

"I'll be fine," she said, but her eyes were closed.

"After my guys set up the security system, we can circle by Graceway to look for the flash drive. How's that sound?"

"Logical," she said, her voice tired and resigned. "It sounds very logical." And within minutes her breathing had slowed to the steady rhythm of sleep.

"We're here."

Ella's eyes blinked opened as Roman parked the SUV. She sat up, surprised she had fallen asleep on the short drive. She had the beginnings of a massive headache, and she was parched. "Wow. I must be more tired than I thought." She looked at the clock, realizing she had missed her morning dose of meds.

"You've been through a lot," Roman said. "Hang tight for a sec."

He stepped out of the vehicle and came around to her side, opening the door for her and keeping an eye on their surroundings. "Once I get you settled, I need to go back to my place for a few hours," he told her, staying close at her heels as they approached the house. "I'll introduce you to the guys before I leave."

The front door opened before they reached the stoop and a striking man in a sharp dark suit filled the doorway. At least six-three, he looked every inch like a high-profile personal body-guard. Minus the sunglasses. Ella supposed he didn't need them on a day like today.

He extended a hand and offered a dimpled smile that killed the intimidation factor and made her instantly at ease. "Ms. Camden, pleased to meet you. I'm Hunter Knox."

"Nice to meet you," she returned as he stepped back for her to enter.

"And this is Luke Everett," Roman said as another man offered a handshake. "He's Triss's older brother." Luke was clean-cut and Roman's height, and offered a brighter smile than any she'd see on his sister's face.

"Triss is impressive," she told him, and his smile widened even more.

"I'm pretty proud of her," he said. It struck her that he seemed to have a fatherly sense of pride in his little sister.

"We'll be working day-to-day for now," Roman explained. "Hunter and Luke will take days until Friday. Triss and I will be here for the night shift. With the cameras we're installing today, we won't need an outside surveillance team. Sound good?" he asked.

She nodded. It sounded better than good. It sounded like the entire weight of the world had been lifted off her shoulders. "Thank you. I'll be in my room if you need me."

She stepped into the kitchen first and took her meds, hoping she'd start feeling better when they kicked in.

"Good thinking," she heard Roman say as she passed the living room. He stepped back from the surveillance table Hunter and Luke had set up with monitors. "It's better this way," he added with a nod of approval.

A memory hit. So vivid it may as well have been yesterday.

"It's better this way," Roman said, his gaze steady on hers, sadness and conviction in his eyes. "You can't pass this up. And we're...we're just not holding up, Ell."

Her throat ached from holding back the sob that threatened. They weren't holding up. They hadn't been for months since Brooklyn's murder. Grieving brought out the worst in both of them. Grieving tied with memories. And guilt.

"I know," she whispered. But if it was really better, why did it hurt so much?

He pulled her close, the faded scent of his cologne imprinting her memory. She breathed it in, closed her eyes and soaked in the solid comfort of his chest. Then he let go and walked away.

Ella turned down the hall toward her bedroom and shut the door behind her, pressing away the memories as she replaced her funeral attire with an old pair of jeans and a soft, long-sleeved T-shirt. She pulled out her phone and sat at the little makeshift desk in the corner, turning on her computer. Time to get some names on paper so she would have something else to give Officer Goodson when he arrived.

She called Autumn first, but the call went to voice mail, so she left a message and then sent an email to Holly on the off chance she had any insight. Finally, she called Bethany, who she'd been avoiding since their last conversation—when she'd confided in her sister about the car tailing her, and Bethany had responded by urging Ella to go back to the doctor.

Bethany answered on the second ring. "Hey, Ella, everything okay?" she asked, her voice serious and thick with concern.

Ella's defenses were on high alert already, knowing that Bethany fully believed her to be suicidal.

"I'm fine," she said, deciding at that moment not to tell her what had happened the previous night. She'd fill her in another day, when her own emotions weren't so fragile.

"Is Mom okay?"

"No change," Ella said. "I'm actually calling because I decided to get in touch with Roman DeHart for some help."

"Roman?" Bethany didn't even try to hide her surprise. "Wow. What brought that on?"

"I don't feel safe," Ella said simply.

"Oh, Ella, you know that—"

"Hold on," Ella cut in. "I don't want to rehash the past few weeks. But I do need something from you."

"What's that?"

"Roman asked me to compile a list of everyone I can think of who had access to Mom's house since I arrived. Can you tell me who's been helping out around here?"

Bethany sighed. "I really don't see the point."

Ella bit back her anger and kept her voice even. "Humor me?"

Bethany was silent, so Ella decided on a new tactic.

"Look, whether or not you believe I'm mentally stable, at least I'll have protection around me 24/7 for a while," she pointed out, forcing her tone to be neutral. "And if there's something to be found, Roman will help me find it. If not, all you did was give me a few names so we can rule out possible perpetrators."

"Fine," Bethany said testily. "Let's see…obviously, most of the neighbors had keys. Monica, in the rancher. Ted, on the other side. And… I can't remember her name… I think it's Nelly or Nina or something—the cat lady across the street."

"Nadia?"

"Right. Nadia." Bethany sighed audibly again.

"Mom's had a lot of help, Ella. This list could get pretty long."

Ella tried not to let her sister's words get to her. Were they a passive-aggressive dig at the fact that Ella hadn't been there for their mom even remotely as much as perfect strangers had been? She couldn't dwell on it.

"I'm just writing down every name I can find, for now," she said. "Continue."

Quite a while later, Ella stared at the list of sixteen people who'd had verifiable access to her mom's house. They had taken care of Isaac, taken out trash and helped with lawn and house maintenance. They'd dropped off meals and stocked the fridge and cabinets. And these were just the people Bethany knew about from the past few months.

In addition to the three neighbors, four teens from the church had helped quite a bit. Then there was Autumn, JT, Lacey, the pastor and his wife and son, two other friends, and of course, Marilynn, who was obviously not a suspect anymore.

Would any of them have motive for murder? The idea was ludicrous.

Ella's mind went back to the flash drive. Would her attacker really have taken it from her purse? How would he have known it was there?

She reviewed her memory of last night. She was sure she'd slipped the flash drive into her purse. Yes. She'd zipped it into that inside pocket so it wouldn't fall out. Or was she mixing memories again?

She flipped on the lamp next to her bed, its light casting over the white-and-green floral quilt. She moved to the dresser, which sat flush against the wall, its empty surface just a little dusty. Even as she searched her laptop case and the desk drawers, she shivered at the thought of her attacker doing just that. Her gaze roved the room.

The nightstand held an old lamp and nothing else. Hamper, half full. Blinds still closed tight. Nothing out of place, unless you counted Mom's crafting table, which Ella had moved to one corner, stacking and organizing all its supplies as best as she could and clearing a work space for herself. No flash drive.

Her attacker must have taken it. Why?

She sat on the edge of the bed. Headache flaring, she pressed her forehead into her hands for a few minutes, eyes scrunched shut.

The low whir of a drill filled the empty quiet, and Ella lifted her head, suddenly disoriented. She recognized the rising confusion but couldn't stop it. She must have hired someone to do some work in the house. Panic welled up. She should stay put, wait for it to pass. But the whirring continued and her own stubbornness forced her up from the bed. She opened the door and padded down the hallway to the kitchen.

"Everything okay?" a male voice asked.

Ella froze at the end of the hall, face-to-face with a very tall man holding a power drill and looking only vaguely familiar.

She stared at him, her mind suddenly, horribly, blank. He wore an immaculate suit and an easy smile, but she couldn't place his face in her memory. Still, she had the inexplicable sense that she should know him. That there was a reason he was in her mother's house.

"Sorry," she said, face flushing.

Just on the edge of her memory, she was certain she'd known his name. Now he was unfamiliar and out of place. Instinct told her she could trust him. This one was on her side. But rising panic stirred up doubt.

"Something wrong?" he asked, his attention roving over her head toward her room.

"Just need to grab my purse," Ella blurted, skirting around him to the kitchen, adrenaline pumping. She'd been looking for the flash drive—that was right.

The man stayed closed at her heels. "Roman ran home for a few, but let me know if you need anything."

Roman?

Her heart lurched and she turned to face the stranger. She wanted to ask why Roman had been there, but somehow she knew she had to hide her confusion.

It will pass, she reminded herself. But how could she be sure?

"Okay, thanks," she said, hoping he didn't notice the unsteadiness in her voice.

She grabbed her purse and brushed past the stranger as she rushed back down the hall. She heard the man's cell phone ring behind her and his voice as he answered it.

Inside her room, she pushed aside her confusion and her questions about the man in the house, and focused on what she did know: the flash drive was missing. She emptied her entire purse onto the bed, but she knew it wouldn't be there, and it wasn't. Maybe it really was still back at the office. She could go look. But the stranger in the house seemed pretty interested in her whereabouts, and the last thing she wanted was him insisting on accompanying her—especially when her own thoughts didn't make sense.

Something wasn't right. She knew it from the hazy gray cloud in her mind making it difficult to think. She should lie down and wait for the confusion to pass. But even as the thought swept through, she grabbed her cell phone and searched the room for a spare pair of shoes. Her mother's old slippers peeked out from under the bed. Ella slipped her bare feet into them and then peeked down the hall to the garage door.

She stepped into the hall, the slippers silent on the old carpet. The man in her mom's house had moved into the living room, the sound of his voice low as he spoke on his phone.

Slowly, Ella turned the old brass knob on the door at the end of the hall. The hinges creaked and she stilled, heart pounding. But the man didn't appear in the hallway. She slipped through the narrow opening, careful not to open the door any wider than necessary.

The garage was dark, but she didn't dare turn the light on. Her car sat inside, a black shadow. She felt her pocket. No keys. She glanced toward the side door. Two blocks wouldn't take long. She could use a coat, though.

An old, heavy utility coat hung on a peg near a rarely used workbench. She hadn't seen her dad since she was seven. Had her mom really never cleared all his stuff out? She pulled the coat away from the wall and shrugged into it. It smelled of motor oil and sawdust and fit her like an oversize poncho, but as least it would keep her warm.

She tucked her cell phone into a deep pocket, zipped up the coat, and approached the side door, unlocking the knob and unhooking the chain.

Freezing wind whipped in as she pulled the door open and peered outside. Yards in front of her, the Monroes' two-story brick Colonial stared flatly back at her. To her right sat the fat old fir tree she and her sisters had planted years ago and named Piney. And to her left, the street.

She stepped away from the house and sucked

in a quiet breath as icy grass grazed her heels. She looked down. Her mother's tattered panda slippers stared back up at her.

She shook her head and briefly considered letting herself back into the house. But her mind swam, her thoughts on the stranger in the house, confusion twisting her ability to rationalize. She wouldn't get frostbite on a half-mile trek in thirty degrees. She'd let herself into the neighbors' backyard and walk a few houses down before approaching the sidewalk. The fences here were four feet and easy to scale.

She nodded assurance to herself and gently shut the door behind her.

SIX

By the time Graceway was in view, Ella's feet had gone numb and her clarity had returned. Too late to turn around now.

She just needed to check her mom's office. Then she'd know for sure if the flash drive had been stolen. She certainly couldn't trust her own memory.

She carefully climbed the icy porch steps to Graceway, hands grasping the cold, steel railing for stability. She reached out to open the door and her heart sank.

Keys. She hadn't brought them.

She closed her eyes for a brief moment, frustrated. It had taken less than ten minutes to walk here, but she was ready to get warmed up. What had she been thinking, walking out of the house without keys? Or shoes? She shivered, eyeing the keyless entry.

She knew the code, but it wouldn't do her any

good. She'd been the last one to leave the office last night, and she always locked the dead bolt.

She punched in the numbers on the off chance that someone else had come into the office between last night and this afternoon and hadn't locked up. The mechanism clicked and she turned the knob, surprised when the door swung open.

She stepped inside, both relieved and nervous. Had someone been working the weekend? Or had someone been inside who didn't belong?

The lobby was dark and she stood for a moment with the door cracked open behind her, listening. Nothing seemed out of the norm. Besides, Ella had worked long hours alone here the last few Saturdays without any problems.

Cold air blew at her back and since she didn't hear signs of anyone else in the building, she pushed the door closed and slid home the dead bolt. The heat was set low for the weekends, but the building was far warmer than the street outside. She flipped on the lights, bathing the lobby in a welcoming glow, encompassed by pale yellow walls and her sister's landscape photography. Her mom had converted a three-story, brick town home into the office space, which was close to home and about twenty miles from Graceway Residential Center.

The pocket of her coat vibrated and Ella jumped, the quiet hum magnified in the empty building. She pulled the phone out, her adrenaline kicking up a notch when she saw the caller ID. Roman.

Reluctantly, she answered, starting up the stairs, her mother's slippers shuffling along the oak steps.

"Ella, Hunter just called and said you snuck out of the house and walked all the way to Graceway. Alone."

Ella paused in the middle of the stairwell, guilt tugging at her conscience. She should have gone back as soon as she'd realized her mistake. At the very least, she should have called and let the team know where she was going.

"I'm sorry," she said, continuing up the stairs and turning onto the third floor. She started across the narrow open hallway, its wrought-iron banister overlooking the lobby below. "I should have called and—"

"We'll discuss it back at the house," he said, cutting her off. His tone was all-business, and Ella bristled at what she knew was impending censure. The still-wet rubber soles of her slippers squeaked along the hardwood floor. "I'm almost to Graceway and Hunter's out on the porch," Roman continued.

"Wait—he followed me here?" Ella asked, surprised and embarrassed that she hadn't even realized.

"You hired Shield for a reason," Roman said, an edge in his voice. "I assumed you understood the first rule of employing protection detail—never go anywhere without them."

"I do understand," she told him, still put off by his tone. "And it won't happen again," she added. She'd explain what had happened later. "Just give me two minutes and I'll be out. Hunter can wait in his car so he doesn't freeze." She'd reached the door to her mom's office, where she'd set up shop over the past several weeks.

"No way. Either you come down and open the door or he'll break a window to get in."

Would he really? She hesitated, her hand on the doorknob. She didn't need Hunter shadowing her as she looked for a flash drive she was 99 percent sure she was not going to find. But dealing with a broken window sounded even less appealing.

"Okay, I'll let him—"

The office door swung inward and Ella screamed as a masked figure barreled toward her.

"Ella!" Roman's voice blared through the phone as she spun away, running across the landing toward the stairs. The intruder snagged her coat, yanking her back. Frantic, she twisted against his grip, her phone dropping to the floor as she fumbled for the zipper to escape. An arm latched around her middle, the grip eerily familiar. She screamed again, just as a gloved hand clasped over her mouth. Black leather gloves. Like last night.

Her attacker dragged her backward, her slippers sliding off, her bare feet skidding along polished floors.

She clawed at his arms, the movement futile against his brute strength.

A loud pounding broke through the struggle. Coming from downstairs.

"Ella!"

Roman!

Hot cigarette breath huffed near her ear and she realized she had another weapon she could use. She slammed her head backward, hoping to get a solid hit to his nose.

The man growled a curse, his grip shifting, and Ella wrenched away, stumbling forward into a run. She didn't make it two steps before he jumped her from behind, sending her to the ground. Her chin smacked the floor hard, pain jarring through her body, just as a loud crash of glass sounded from downstairs.

A hand snatched her head up by the hair, a thick cord of some sort along the front of her throat.

No!

The noose cinched, closing her airway in an instant. Panicked, she tried to grab it, but the cord held fast. She couldn't breathe, felt her skin growing hot. *Please, God, help me.*

Her ears were ringing and she started to fade.

"Ella!" Roman's shout echoed from somewhere downstairs. She just had to hold on a few more seconds, but darkness blanketed her mind, her limbs weak and still…

And suddenly the pressure released. Ella's face smacked full-weight against the floor, nose-first, and tears streamed down her cheeks.

She dragged in a sharp, ragged breath and opened her eyes as Roman appeared at the top of the stairs.

"Ella!" He was at her side in an instant, crouched next to her. "Are you hurt?" His hands settled on her shoulders, his gaze scanning her for injury.

"No." Her voice was raspy, her vocal cords tender.

He stood, grabbing her arm and pulling her up next to him.

A window scraped open across the hall from her mother's office and Hunter flew past the two of them toward the movement. Roman pointed to her mom's office where the door still hung open. "Barricade yourself in there. Call 9-1-1."

"What are you—?"

"Now." He nudged her into the room and she turned, closing the door just in time to see him grab his gun from its holster.

She locked the flimsy doorknob, heart knocking, hands shaking. She'd wanted to tell Roman to come in with her. To wait with her for help to arrive. But she knew him. Even after all these years, she knew him.

Knew he wouldn't hide out when a predator was within reach. She also knew that if she followed him, he'd have the extra responsibility of keeping her safe, which would only add to the risk.

She grabbed the edge of a tall bookshelf and shoved it across the floor in front of the door. Not heavy enough. The door wouldn't hold against a body slam. She'd push the desk over. She swiveled around to cross the room—and bashed her foot into hard metal.

She gasped, grabbing her foot and crouching low.

A ladder?

She stared at the offending ladder leg for half a second, grimacing in pain. Had someone been changing a lightbulb?

No time. She pushed herself to stand. She needed to call for help and—

She stopped cold.

A thick, bristly rope hung from the rafters, tightly secured with several loops near the ceiling. And dangling from the end was what could only be…a noose.

She took a step back, her hand touching the tender skin at her neck where the cord had been. Had she walked in on another setup? Another attempt to make her death look like a suicide?

But he couldn't have known she'd come.

Couldn't have known she'd be the first person to come upon the scene.

Or had he?

She'd come every Saturday without fail. Worked alone for hours on end. Had he been watching?

Banging sounded from beyond the door. Not gun shots. Footsteps? The fire escape? There was one outside the office across the hall. Had the guy escaped that way?

The questions yanked her back into the moment and she skirted the ladder, grabbing hold of the phone on her mom's desk and dialing with shaky fingers.

"Nine-one-one. Where is your emergency?"

Ella spouted out the address and explained about the intruder. All the while, she stared at the noose hanging limp.

For her?

There seemed no other explanation. Her gaze traveled up the thick rope to where it had been expertly bound and knotted to a ceiling beam. Something white peeked out from between the knot and the beam. She edged her way toward the noose, trying to get a better look.

"The police are on the way, Ella," the dispatcher said, sounding much less urgent than Ella thought she should. "Stay on the line with me."

What was it? A paper of some sort? It was tucked under one loop of the rope.

"Ella?" the dispatcher prodded.

"Yes. I'm here," Ella said, stepping onto the first rung of the ladder, the phone sandwiched between her jaw and shoulder. She took another step and looked up. The A-frame ceiling was high and her legs were less than steady on the ladder. She held tightly to the rungs and continued her ascent.

"Do you hear the intruder now?" the dispatcher asked. "Is he still in the building?"

"I don't hear anything," Ella said, reaching the second highest rung and pausing to listen. "I don't know if he's still here."

But she heard sirens. Help would be there soon.

"The police are almost there," the dispatcher said. "Where are you located inside the building?"

"I'm on the third floor, the office facing the street."

"Just stay where you are. Let them come to you."

"Okay." Ella didn't have any intention of leaving the office until an officer was standing right in front of her. She reached up toward the rafters and tried to grasp the edge of the folded piece of paper that had been wedged under the rope.

She couldn't quite reach it. She needed just another couple of inches. She eyed the top step of the ladder, fingers tingling with nervous energy. Her balance hadn't been good since the injury last month. She should just wait. Anyway, she shouldn't touch evidence. Common sense prevailed and she grabbed the ladder again to make her way down.

She'd moved one foot down to the next rung when a loud rapping sounded at the door. Her heart lurched.

"Ella? It's Roman!"

"Hold on!" she yelled over the wail of the sirens. She took shaky steps down the ladder and quickly pushed the bookshelves out of the way, opening the door for Roman.

He stepped inside, his hands coming to her arms. "Are you okay?" he asked.

"Fine. Just shaky," she lied, wanting nothing more than to throw her arms around him and feel somehow safe again.

"We didn't catch the guy," Roman said. "I don't know how he—"

He stopped midsentence, his attention suddenly fixed beyond Ella. On the ladder and noose.

"It's not what it looks like—" she started to explain. But as he wrapped his arms around her, words failed her. He pressed a soft kiss to the top of her head, and she leaned into his chest, reassured by the steady beat of his heart.

"Ella?" a voice called from the phone at their feet. Neither of them moved to pick it up. She thought she'd memorized his embrace, but she'd forgotten. She'd forgotten how safe and how warm and how loved she always felt tucked into the strength of his arms.

"Hey, boss." Hunter appeared in the doorway and Ella and Roman quickly separated. "The rest of the building's clear," Hunter said as if it was perfectly normal to find his boss embracing a client.

"Good work," Roman said.

"These yours?" Hunter asked with an amused grin, handing Ella the panda slippers.

"Afraid so," she admitted. "Thanks." Just as she shoved her cold feet back into the slippers, the police barged in downstairs, announcing their presence, footsteps clamoring up the stairs.

Roman moved to the doorway. "In here!" he called.

"Everyone okay?" a voice asked from the hall.

"We're okay, Tyler," Roman said as an officer appeared in the doorway.

He looked from Roman to Ella, and to the noose and ladder in the middle of the room. "What's going on?"

Roman filled the officer in on what had happened, up until the moment he and Hunter had scaled the back fence only to find the guy had disappeared.

"I'm thinking he had a car waiting," Hunter added.

Ella leaned against the desk behind her, shoulders sagging with relief. At least there'd been witnesses this time. Part of her story, both men could corroborate. Otherwise, all she had to show for herself was a bizarre decision to walk to the office in slippers without telling anyone, and then a noose in her mom's office without any explanation.

Officer Goodson pointed to the noose in question.

"What about this?" he asked.

"I don't know how it got here," Ella said.

"Anyone else in the building?" the officer asked.

Ella shook her head no.

"Did you get a good look at the guy?"

"It happened so fast," Ella answered. "He was wearing all black. He had on a black ski mask. I only saw his eyes. They looked black, too."

"I only got a glimpse of his back," Roman said. "He was wearing a thin black jacket."

"Sit tight for just a minute," Tyler said. He moved back toward the doorway, talking into his radio.

Roman crossed the room and pulled the desk chair away from the wall, dragging it toward Ella. "Why don't you sit?" She was leaning so far into the desk, she was in danger of sliding to the floor.

She sat in the rolling chair, hands clasped in her lap. She was a sight, from the enormous old jacket she'd donned to the dingy panda slippers on her feet.

"What were you thinking?" he asked. "You

didn't tell anyone where you were going. If Hunter and Luke hadn't been so astute, we could have had a very different outcome."

She could be dead. But he didn't say it. The Ella he'd grown up with was smart enough to know it, and the regret flashing in her eyes convinced him she did.

"I'm sorry," she said softly. "I had one of my memory lapses again and—"

"Okay," Tyler said, reentering the room. He had a pad of paper and pen in hand. "We've got men fanning out around the building and down the street behind us. In the meantime, let's start at the beginning so I can get some more information."

Roman listened as Ella recounted the events of the afternoon. When he heard about the memory lapse and the missing flash drive, he could almost see how she'd jumped into a dangerous decision.

He eyed the noose as Ella described the attack. Anyone with half a brain would know that Ella hadn't had enough time to rig that rope up. Mere minutes had passed between Ella entering the building and Roman and Hunter breaking in a window.

"So, the noose was here when you ran into the office?" Tyler was prodding. Roman had known the guy for a long time. He was sharp and would get a thorough report. Then he'd pull out all the stops to solve the case.

"Yes. I called 9-1-1, and then tried to get up close because I saw something up there. A note, maybe. I couldn't quite reach it."

"Good. Better that you didn't touch anything."

"My prints will be all over the ladder, though," Ella said.

Tyler said nothing, scribbling more notes on his pad. Then he stepped back and looked up the length of the rope. "I see what you're talking about. We'll get an evidence team in here and find out what it is."

His attention moved to Roman. "In the meantime, you can take Ms. Camden home. Let me walk you guys out."

It had started to snow, and it looked like the kind that would stick. Unusual for Maryland in November.

Roman let Ella into his SUV and shut the door.

"I'll finish up here and come by in a bit with a photographer," Tyler said. "We'll need to get some photos of the marks on her neck."

So, Tyler had noticed, too. The marks were barely visible, but Roman suspected they'd darken fast.

They shook hands as they parted ways and Roman got in the driver's seat, shutting the door to the cold and blasting the heat. Putting the SUV in reverse, he caught a glimpse of Ella huddled down in the seat, nearly hidden inside the old dusty work coat.

"Cold?" he asked, turning the heat up.

"I can't seem to get warm enough," she said, her voice tight. She tugged the coat tighter, a tremor in her hands.

At a stoplight, Roman turned his attention fully to her. It wasn't just her hands that were shaking. The edge of the coat shivered, her face set in a deep frown. It wasn't the cold doing that to her. It was shock. Vulnerability. Fear. He'd seen it more than once in the past four years since he and his dad had started Shield together.

In a different time, he would have reached across the console for her hand. But if he did that now…he'd be lost.

He knew that about himself. Years had flashed by and they had both changed, but his heart still beat a steady rhythm toward hers.

Their connection had ultimately been their destruction. Two passionate hearts broken in grief and guilt when Brooklyn was murdered. He cleared his throat, feeling that old regret rising. Hindsight showed him the words they'd exchanged had been a grief response. But then they'd separated and time had marched on like it had a habit of doing. He'd assumed Ella had found happiness in her career. By now, he'd imagined her married with a couple of kids. That's where he'd imaged he'd be, too.

It hadn't worked out that way. Shield had become his life. His clients, his family. For a long time it had felt right. It had felt like enough. Lately, though, he'd been fighting a sense of emptiness. It'd started right about the day his brother Chase had gotten married, come to think of it. It had been a long time since Roman had been in a relationship, and even longer since he'd felt that spark of connection and friendship with a woman.

No one had ever come close to Ella. He hadn't wanted to admit it, but there it was—and a useless admission at that. He'd lost her six years ago and it had been his own fault. The passing of time may have softened the ache of regret, but was it powerful enough to mend their relationship? Even if it was, Ella was in a vulnerable position, and Roman wouldn't take advantage of that by dredging up the past.

Even if the thought of losing her today had made his heart stop.

Even if holding her had reminded him of how perfectly she fit in his arms.

And especially because he'd caused enough hurt in Ella's life, and he'd never be able to guarantee a happy ending.

SEVEN

The snow flurries had thickened to heavy flakes, sticking to the grass and bushes as Roman and Ella wordlessly approached Julia Camden's house together. As Roman reached for the front door, a car sounded behind them. He turned toward the street. Next to him, Ella groaned.

He passed her a sideways glance as he watched the navy Lexus slowly pull up behind his vehicle. "Unwelcome guest?"

"Pastor Wright."

Curious. Seemed like the pastor would be a welcomed visitor, but Roman didn't personally know the guy, had only spent a handful of minutes speaking with him at the reception.

Pastor Wright smiled warmly as he crossed the lawn, grass crunching under his shoes. "Saw some police cars in front of Graceway," he said. "I tried to call you, Ella, but got your voice mail." He hesitated, his attention swerving to Roman for a moment. "Thought I'd swing by the house and check on you. Did I catch you at a bad time?"

"Not at all," Ella said as Luke opened the door to them. "Come on in." Her voice was genuine and welcoming, but her body language screamed exhaustion, so Roman moved between the pastor and the open door.

"Actually," he said, "it might be better if you came back tomorrow. Ella's been through the wringer."

"Sure," the pastor said, staying put at the foot of the porch. "Feel better, Ella," he added, sending her a quick wave.

She thanked him for understanding and disappeared inside the house, but the pastor didn't make a move to leave. "What happened?" he asked.

"She was attacked and nearly strangled."

If Hank Wright was shocked by that revelation, he didn't show it. "Did they catch the guy?" he asked.

"Not yet."

The pastor looked beyond Roman into the house. Ella had already made herself scarce. His attention shifted to Roman then, his gaze probing. "And…" he hesitated. "You're sure there really was an attacker?"

"What do you mean?" Roman knew what the guy was getting at, but he planned to make him spell it out anyway.

The pastor rubbed his jaw. "There have been a lot of strange…incidents since Ella came home," he said. He lowered his voice. "I'm worried about her."

"Let me worry about her," Roman said coolly. "We've got a plan in place. If this guy goes after her again, we'll be ready."

The pastor frowned. "That's just the thing. I'm afraid the only person who wants to hurt Ella… is herself."

Roman rocked back on his heels to keep from doing what he was tempted to do—walk into the house and shut the door in the pastor's face. It wasn't that he didn't appreciate the guy's concern. He didn't like the approach.

"This time, there were witnesses," Roman said. "I'm one of them." He'd seen her attacker with his own eyes, and the bruises forming on her neck would convince any doubter. But Roman didn't feel compelled to fill the pastor in on the situation. "If you don't mind…" He gestured to the house, and the pastor nodded.

"I'll visit again after things have settled," he said, turning back toward his car.

Roman let himself into Julia's house, locking up and setting the alarm. Luke had completed the system install while they were at Graceway. Good. It would be even more difficult for Ella to leave the house unnoticed now. The chime would go off every time a window or door was opened.

Voices carried into the living room and he made his way to the kitchen. Ella had taken a seat at the old, round, oak table, and Hunter was leaning against the kitchen counter, arms crossed.

"I really am sorry," Ella was saying, her cheeks rosy.

"I'm just glad you're all right," Hunter responded. He met Roman's eyes. "Ella was explaining to me a little more about the brain injury."

The doorbell rang and Isaac let out a series of shrill barks. "Must be Triss," Roman said, crossing back to the front to let Luke's sister in. Isaac appeared at Roman's feet, still yapping as Roman opened the door.

Triss had traded her leggings for a trim pants suit, and her hair was secured in a tight bun. If she wore makeup, he couldn't detect it. She often washed it off before the job, as if to prove she was one of the guys.

She didn't need to. Everyone knew she was one of the best shooters on the Shield team, one of the coolest guards under pressure, one of the fastest runners. She was passionate about the work and Roman was glad to have her on board. He particularly appreciated being able to pull her into cases like this one, where his team was setting up in the home of a female client.

She unwrapped her scarf and peered down at Isaac.

"Sorry," Ella said, entering the room behind them. "Once he greets you, he'll stop."

Triss crouched and extended an open palm for the dog to sniff.

Isaac took a few curious whiffs, eyed the latest company, and returned to his spot on the couch.

"For such a little thing, he sure has a big yapper," Hunter said, joining the others. "A built-in alarm system, huh?"

Roman locked the door behind Triss. "Not a reliable one," Roman said. "He didn't make a sound when I came to the house last night."

"True, but he was hurt and hiding," Ella pointed out.

"All the same, I'll take a Shield system any day over a fuzzy little dog," Triss said.

Roman grinned at her matter-of-fact tone. "Looks like you made it just before the snow picked up," he said. "Hope we don't get snowed in."

November snowstorms weren't common in Maryland, but it sure looked like this storm would be a messy one.

Triss held up a grocery bag dangling from her arm. "I brought hot chocolate." She didn't smile, just swept past him and set the bag on an empty space on the kitchen counter.

She was too young to be so serious, so driven, but Roman had a feeling big things would come her way. He hoped she'd open her heart to them.

He'd felt an almost brotherly love toward her that matched Luke's, as he'd watched her transform from wayward teenager to grown woman. Watched as Luke had struggled and prayed—even wept—over his worry for her. She'd been on her own journey, though. Just as they all were.

"So, they gave you the night shift," Ella said with a friendly smile toward Triss. "To make sure I don't escape my bedroom in the middle of the night?"

Triss tilted her head to the side and shot a questioning look at Roman. "The alarm's installed, right?"

"Just finished," he confirmed.

Triss nodded. "You won't be able to," she said, staring flatly at Ella.

"To what?" Ella asked, frowning.

"Escape," Triss answered, nonchalant. "Alarm will sound whenever a door or window opens." Roman knew her well enough by now to recognize that she wasn't trying to be rude or accusatory. It was just Triss's way. She called things as she saw them and she always spoke truth.

He would have believed the comments had bounced right off of Ella except for the pinking of her ears. Still, he couldn't tell if Ella was angry or embarrassed. Maybe she was both.

Ella peered out at the snow through the back door. "If I try to go out in this mess, I hope someone will stop me." She turned back to the group and flashed a sheepish grin.

Roman was glad to see the shock had started to wear off, and Ella was regaining her composure and her sense of humor. "Speaking of going out in this mess... Hunter, you'd better get moving before the roads get too bad."

"My sitter's pretty flexible... I can stick around," Hunter offered, and Roman knew he was good for it. He also knew Hunter wanted the chance to make up for the afternoon's close call.

"You'll be more help to the team rested up for tomorrow," Roman said. "Go home to your family. Just keep your phone on."

"You got it."

"Here," Triss said, rustling around in the grocery bag she'd brought. She pulled out a small box of hot cocoa mix, tore off the top and produced three packets for Hunter. "I got the kind with extra marshmallows."

Hunter grinned. "Thanks. The kids'll love it." Hunter's wife had died two years ago and he'd been raising his son and daughter alone since.

Roman walked him out and reset the alarm, then turned back to the quiet house. The women weren't in the kitchen anymore. He checked the monitors for the surveillance cameras. Two monitors showed four angles each. If someone tried to approach the house, they'd see it coming.

He crossed the room and peered down the hall, heard the shower start up.

Triss reentered the hall from the garage. "They've got a few bags of salt in there we could use on the porch steps," she said. "Ella's taking a shower," she added, skirting past Roman and parking herself on the arm of the old brown recliner. "So, what happened today? Those bruises…"

Roman filled Triss in quickly. Per her nature, she didn't make much of a response. When he was through, she nodded. "So, the attacker is no longer fictional."

"Doesn't look like it," Roman said.

"Good."

"Ella may not feel the same way," Roman said, baffled. He didn't always follow Triss's logic.

She shrugged. "I like her. I don't want her sent off to a mental institution."

"It'd be a safer situation than being hunted," Roman pointed out.

"Not if she's suicidal."

She had a point there.

Triss stood and headed for the kitchen. "Want some hot chocolate?"

"I'll pass, thanks." The only hot chocolate that tempted Roman was his mother's from-scratch recipe, topped with frothy whipped cream and a drizzle of hot fudge.

Triss started to fill the teapot with water. It was

old stainless steel, just like the one from his child-hood. A memory swept in and sucker punched him. He turned away and moved to the window, watching the snow gather along the edges of the garden bed and pile up on the overgrown ever-green bushes.

His mother set a mug in front of him. It was white with a jolly snowman and a silly penguin. She set an identical one in front of twelve-year-old Ella Camden. Ella reached to grab hers but Roman's mother held up a hand. "Not yet," she said with a gentle smile. Then she pulled out the can of whipped cream and grabbed the chocolate syrup from the microwave where she'd heated it.

He watched Ella's face change as she observed the hot chocolate ritual. Shock and exhaustion faded from her expression, color returning to her cheeks and a light entering her eyes. Her long, coppery hair hung in disarray, damp from the snow, her freckles standing out against her pale skin. His mother sprayed whipped cream into each of their steaming mugs, sprinkled some cin-namon and then drizzled on hot fudge. She didn't often make her homemade chocolate brew, but tonight had definitely called for it.

"Now," his mother said. "This is what a sur-vivor and a hero drink after a night like tonight."

Snow had been falling that night, too. Roman could see it all in slow motion. The neighborhood kids had been out in the mess, having snowball fights and building misshapen snowmen.

The dog had come from out of nowhere. One minute Ella had been raising her arm to toss a snowball and the next she'd been falling backward, her screams echoing down the street.

Roman had known Ella for years, but they'd bonded that night, when a hundred-pound stray had grabbed hold of her elbow and seemed to be hungry for more.

The teapot started to hum and Roman pulled the front curtains closed.

"I'm just going to take my mug down the hall and wait for Ella," Triss said, pouring the water into her powdery mix. "Feel free to…do your thing."

He suppressed a grin of amusement. "You could always join me…"

"You have a better chance of God listening without me in the room," she said lightly, a hint of a smile curving her lips. But he saw the sadness there.

He opened his mouth to remind her about forgiveness and grace, but she put up a hand. "I know, I know. Grace, and all that. For now, you go ahead." She disappeared down the hall.

Roman sighed. Triss had a past she deeply regretted. He didn't know many of the details, but she carried a burden she didn't feel she could let go of.

He walked to the front door, placed his right hand on the fading paint and bowed his head. As was his custom, he prayed protection over the house. He prayed that all evil would be barred from entry. He prayed for health and alertness for his team and their clients. And tonight, he spent a few extra minutes praying for the two women in the Camden house who seemed to be weighed down with a pain only God could lift.

He let his hand slide away from the old front door, the rough, peeling paint a testimony to the many years of life spent in the home. He stared at the door for a moment, remembering Ella opening it to him years ago. She'd asked him to her prom—as a friend, she'd said, because she didn't have anyone she wanted to go with. But somehow he'd known it was more than that.

A shuffle of movement sounded behind him and he turned to find Ella at the threshold between the hall and the kitchen. "Everything okay?" she asked.

He could only manage a nod as his memory of seventeen-year-old Ella in the poufy, pink, ballerina-style dress merged with the vision in front of him. She was wearing a pair of sky-blue leggings with a cozy-looking white, long-sleeved T-shirt, her hair towel-dried and naturally wavy.

"Triss said there was hot chocolate," she said, stepping into the kitchen. He heard the rip of the packet, the gush of water pouring from the teapot.

Minutes later, Ella reappeared in the doorway, one shoulder leaning against the door frame, mug in hand.

"Nothing has ever compared to that hot chocolate your mom made years ago," she said. "Remember that?"

"It was a memorable night."

"What was?" Triss asked, gliding into the kitchen.

"When I was in the sixth grade, Roman saved me from a dog attack."

Triss's eyebrows shot up. "What happened?"

Ella sipped the cocoa and then set it down. "The dog came out of nowhere and latched on." She pushed the right sleeve of her shirt up past her elbow and turned her arm to show off the scars.

Triss blew out a breath. "Looks like the dog wanted to rip your arm off."

"I think he could have. Roman jumped on top of him while all of our friends screamed their heads off and went running."

"My dad ran out and shot his rifle in the air. The dog took off," Roman said.

"And then your mom served you guys some kind of dreamy hot chocolate?" Triss asked with disbelief. "A trip to the hospital may have been more imperative."

Ella laughed at Triss's technical take on the hot-chocolate story. "We couldn't get out. We were in the middle of a snowstorm. They wrapped my arm and we had to wait for a plow to escort an ambulance."

"You two have known each other a long time," Triss noted, pulling over a dining chair and taking a seat.

"That's why I asked for his help," Ella said, feeling Roman's gaze on her. "He's good at what he does. I wanted the best."

"You want my best, you're going to have to trust me like you used to," Roman said, and Ella's gaze cut to him. "No going anywhere alone."

"I didn't rebelliously decide to leave the house," Ella said quietly, anger bubbling up. "I told you, I had a memory lapse again. It's hard to explain what happens when—"

"I get it, Ell," Roman said, cutting her off. But then his tone gentled. "That's why we've put in the safeguards of the alarm system and surveillance cams." He grinned. "You asked for help, and there's no going back now."

"I wasn't planning to go back," Ella said.

"And no Ethiopia trip." He turned resolute eyes to her.

"What Ethiopia trip?" Triss asked. "When is it?"

"There's no trip," Roman repeated.

"Early Monday," Ella answered.

"How long?" Triss questioned.

"Three days, plus travel. I'd be back by Friday."

"It won't work, Ella," Roman said. "I can't get a team together on such short notice for a trip to Africa."

"I could skip a few classes," Triss suggested, but Roman was already shaking his head.

"No way. I appreciate the offer, but this job is not getting in the way of your school."

"The threat is here," Ella said, frustration rising. "I doubt he'd follow me across the world."

"There's a chance he would," Roman pointed out. "Look, I'm just suggesting you postpone for a while."

"I feel like the trip can't really wait," Ella insisted. She didn't have any facts to back up the statement, but her gut instinct told her there had to have been an important reason she'd booked the trip in the first place.

A movement flickered from the screen overlooking the front yard. A police cruiser pulled up. No flashing lights.

"Must be Tyler," Roman said. "I'll let him in."

Officer Goodson looked like a man on a mission as he got out of his squad car and marched across the snowy yard, head down to the wind. Another man exited the car from the passenger side and jogged up next to him, a heavy black bag slung over his shoulder.

Ella stood to the side as Roman opened the door for the men. Snow speckled the shoulders of Officer Goodson's black uniform jacket and the brim of his tan hat. He stomped his boots on the faded welcome mat and removed his hat at the door, brushing it off before stepping inside.

"Roman," he said with a slight smile as the other man stepped in quietly behind him. "Ms. Camden." He looked serious, his gaze catching on her face for an extra moment. He glanced at Triss.

"This is my partner for the evening," Roman said, introducing Triss.

Officer Goodson shook Triss's hand and motioned to the guy next to him. "This is our department photographer, Randy Palmer."

Roman led the small group into the living room and everyone took a seat.

Officer Goodson's gaze moved to the screens. "I see you've got a system set up already."

"We started this morning," Roman told him.

The officer nodded, his gaze settling on Ella again.

She felt like squirming under his observation, but she sat up instead, moving a pillow behind her back so she wouldn't slouch into the old couch.

"We didn't find any signs of the attacker. No signs of forced entry, either." He paused, as if allowing time for her to fess up to a fabricated story. Ella pressed her lips together.

"Someone was in there," Roman said calmly. "I saw the guy running down that fire escape and scaling the fence." He gestured toward Ella. "And you can see the evidence he left on her neck."

"Those are some dark bruises," the officer agreed. "That's why I brought Randy with me. We'd like to take photographs for evidence."

"Sure," Ella said, but frowned, circling back to their previous conversation. "So that's it?" she asked. "Nothing could be found?"

"Not yet. It'll take a while to wrap up the scene. Now, you were planning to come by my office earlier—you have my undivided attention. Tell me what's been going on."

Ella accepted a glass of water Roman handed to her and started at the beginning. She told Officer Goodson about her mom's cancer, and her car accident—and the state of Graceway when Ella had arrived. She recounted all three attacks on her life and spoke about the car following her. She told him about the computer virus and the missing flash drive.

An hour ticked by on the clock above the television. All the while, the officer took notes and asked clarifying questions. When she finally finished, she sagged against the couch, emotionally drained.

Officer Goodson looked over his notes. "Thank you, Ella. This paints a pretty detailed picture and you're right—the common denominator seems to be Graceway."

"I'm working on a list of people who had access to Graceway and also to my mom's house," she added.

"That would be helpful. In the meantime, stay close to home," he advised.

"Of course," she said, figuring now was not the time to mention the trip to Ethiopia. She needed to find a way to convince Roman about it. Hopefully, if she could get her hands on the recovered files, she might find some clues about why she had scheduled the trip in the first place.

"Let's get these pictures taken care of, then," the officer said.

Ella patiently stood for the photos, lifting her chin as directed so Randy could get good pictures of the bruising. Her face flamed under Roman's watch. At least he had seen the attacker. But he still seemed just a little unsure about her. A little on guard. She supposed he had a right to be, considering she'd pulled a disappearing act twice now in two days.

"That'll do it," Randy finally said, and began to pack up.

Handshakes were exchanged and as the men moved toward the door, a thought struck Ella. She set a hand on the officer's arm. He turned to her.

"Did you get to that white paper on the beam in my mom's office?" she asked.

He hesitated then nodded curtly.

"Was it…anything?" she asked, a chill of foreboding snaking down her spine.

"It was a suicide note, Ella," he said. "Signed by you."

EIGHT

Ella watched, numb, as Officer Goodson and the photographer climbed into the cruiser and pulled away from the house.

A suicide note...signed by you.

The officer's words echoed in her mind, sending a current of fear down her spine.

The evidence would be processed, he'd told her, along with any prints the police had found, and she could expect to get a glimpse of the note at a later date. That's all he would give her, and he'd watched her carefully as he'd spoken. What did he think he could read in her eyes? Guilt? A secret?

"Let's go ahead and lock up," Roman said next to her, and she stepped back to let him shut the door. He slid the new dead bolt into place and moved to reset the alarm.

She'd spotted him at the door earlier that evening, hand on the worn paint, head down. Praying? She didn't remember Roman as an overly religious guy.

He stepped away from the door and Ella started for the hallway. She should turn in. Being close to Roman brought back all sorts of feelings she wasn't prepared to face. It had taken years to move on after leaving Maryland. Years before the memory of him could flit through her mind without the sharp ache of regret. The last thing she needed was to reopen the wound.

"This place brings back a lot of memories," he said.

She paused, turning back to him.

He glanced around the room, a mix of nostalgia and sadness in his expression. Then his eyes met hers.

"Prom night," he said softly and grinned.

"You two went to the prom together?" Triss asked, sweeping into the room and settling onto the couch.

Ella laughed. The woman had supersonic hearing. "We did."

"Let me guess," Triss said, cocking her head to the side. "You wore a poufy pink concoction and he wore a bow tie."

The memory poured into Ella's heart, tingling with emotion. "Pretty close," she said, moving to the bookcase where her mom had stacked photo albums. She grabbed one and brought it over to the couch. Sitting next to Triss, she flipped the hard pages of the album open and her eyes lit on the prom spread.

There they were. Pre-prom friends. She could almost feel the warm weight of his hand at her waist, could see her mom taking the photos as her heart thrummed with anticipation. Hours later they'd shared their first kiss, a kiss that had been seared into her memory for the rest of her days.

"So, you two were high school sweethearts?" Triss asked as Roman crossed the room to look at the pictures.

"You could say that. Roman graduated a couple years ahead of me," Ella said.

Roman leaned over the album, his hand next to Ella on the arm of the couch. "Look at you," he said. "All decked out in pink."

Ella pored over the photos. One in front of the house, two by the front yard tree. Another in front of Roman's red Mustang convertible.

Roman reached over and pulled the page up, turning to the next before she could stop him. Her breath caught and he stilled beside her.

"What a gang of friends," Triss said, oblivious to the mood change. "But you two definitely won the award for best dressed."

The photo had been taken before the prom at a friend's house, in the backyard, a weeping willow behind the large group.

Ella's eyes zeroed in on one person and she knew Roman's did the same. To their right stood

Brooklyn, Roman's only sister. A couple of years later, she was dead.

Triss let out a short laugh. "You must both be stuck hard in memory lane or something." She started to push the album back to Ella's lap. "I'll leave you to it."

"Sorry, Triss," Roman said as she stood. He pointed to the beaming brunette, hair curled around her shoulders, a satin, teal gown skimming her petite curves. "This is a picture of my sister I hadn't seen in a long time."

Triss stared down at the photo. "Brooklyn, right?"

He nodded.

"Luke told me about her," she said, her tone uncharacteristically soft. "She was beautiful." She pointed to the blond kid next to her. He was wearing a white tux. "That's not—?"

Roman shook his head. "No. That's Pete, an old friend. She met her killer the next year in college."

"He's still in jail?" Triss asked.

"Yes. And he'll stay there, if I have anything to do with it."

Roman's hand swept lightly over the plastic page cover. "That was a good night," he said. "She was happy." He turned to meet Ella's eyes. "So were you."

Her neck warmed under his gaze, memories flooding in. An after-prom bonfire in their friend's backyard, the bright stars of a late spring night. Kids had been running in to change to get into the hot tub, Ella and Roman lingering alone by the warmth of the fire.

"You asked me to prom just as a friend, right, Ella?" Roman asked her as they stared into the waning fire, and her heart sank. She had. But she'd hoped for more.

She nodded, unable to voice the longings of her heart for fear she'd ruin the friendship they did have.

His hand found hers and she smiled, hoping her emotions weren't clear on her face. "That's too bad," he said quietly. "Because I've never wanted to kiss anyone more than I want to kiss you right now."

"What happened to you?" he asked, the question pulling her from the memory.

Ella glanced at the living room windows. Triss had slipped out. "I'm still happy," she said, closing the album and standing. She returned it to the bookshelf.

"You changed after Brooklyn died."

"We both did," she said, turning back to him. "We *all* did," she added.

"True," he said, his eyes dark with memories.

Every vein of their lives had been touched by Brooklyn's death. No one would ever be the same. For years Ella had lamented that fact, but she wouldn't have wanted it any other way. Because she wouldn't have wanted Brooklyn to be forgotten.

Ironic, because it was Brooklyn's memory that had come between Ella and Roman, their shared grief edging them further and further apart each day. She'd blamed herself, and Roman had let her. If he only knew how right he'd been...

"Some changes were for the best," Ella pointed out, walking to the windows under the pretense of checking on the storm as Triss had done. Really, she just needed a little distance from Roman before she let her guard down and her emotions slipped out. "You and your dad grew closer, started Shield. Your mom found a new career."

From what Ella had heard, Mrs. DeHart had spearheaded over a dozen new laws to help protect other domestic violence victims. Ella would have liked to have been involved with that. Instead she'd hightailed it out of the state.

"And you..." Roman said, his voice closer. She turned to find him moving toward her with an unhurried gait that didn't match the intense focus in his eyes. He stopped inches in front of her and all the old feelings surged. She stood rooted to her spot, battling the strongest desire to take one step forward, press her cheek to his chest, slide her arms around his waist.

"You started over," he finished, his dark gaze probing.

Ran away, she corrected him silently.

"Got a new place, a new job, a new life."

Ella shrugged. "But I didn't change all that much in the process. I'm still the same person I was. You can't judge me based on the past couple of days, Roman. This is not my normal."

"What isn't?"

"Hospitalizations. Memory lapses. Paranoia. Needing a bodyguard... It's all been since I came here." She could feel her voice rising in pitch, her anxiety kicking up. Had she taken her medicine this morning? She couldn't remember.

Roman could hear the emotion rise in Ella's tone. "I'll take your word for it," he said in an attempt to reassure her. It was all he could do, but he'd do it with caution.

"It's the strangest thing, Roman."

"What is?"

"I don't remember much of my first few weeks here before I wound up in the hospital, but I remember this strong feeling of anxiety. I have flashes of memory. I remember staying late at Graceway on the computer, going up on the weekends."

"Searching for something?"

She nodded. "That's why I want to get hold of those files. I keep thinking something in there might jog my memory."

"I'll check with Tyler to see if we can go back to Graceway early tomorrow, before church," he suggested. "That way you can check for the flash drive. If it's not there, you can get in touch with TechSavvy on Monday."

"That'll work," Ella said. "It's got to be there," she added. "Why would someone steal it? And how would anyone know it was in my purse?"

Roman considered her words for a moment. "It's possible whoever attacked you at the house last night rummaged through your purse before he left. He may want to know what you've gotten your hands on."

"If it's someone at Graceway, it shouldn't be hard to narrow it down. Staff is pretty low."

"Is that typical?"

"Not that I know of. I mean, my mom's out, obviously. And Marilynn was the secretary. The marketing coordinator gave her two weeks' notice to Marilynn while I was in the hospital. By the time I got back to Graceway, she was gone. I haven't even started a search for candidates to take her place. Our accountant, Wes Bentley, is hit or miss lately—shows up to work late or not at all. I haven't had the time to deal with it. JT's about the only constant fixture at Graceway. Autumn's in and out."

"That's not a lot of people to keep the organization running," Roman commented.

"There are more people," Ella explained. "We've got a dozen or so over at the residential program, and at least that many in Ethiopia at our sister programs. But, no—we don't have enough people to run Graceway from headquarters."

"Sounds like a real mess," Roman said. "It also sounds like we need to dig deeper into Graceway's finances. What did Marilynn—?"

"White Honda Pilot just pulled up," Triss said, appearing at the edge of the living room.

Roman moved toward the surveillance screens and Ella followed him. "It's Autumn," she said as her friend emerged from the car. But instead of closing the door, Autumn turned back to the car and leaned inside, then came out again, two steaming boxes of pizza in her hands.

"Were you expecting her?" Roman asked, moving toward the front door.

"She drops by a lot," Ella said.

Roman started to unbolt the door as the doorknob jiggled. He opened the door to a puzzled Autumn, hanging on to the pizza boxes and her old key to the house.

"We changed the locks," Ella said.

"That explains it," Autumn replied with a grin, shoving the keys into her oversize turquoise-leather purse. "I brought pizza," she added, stating the obvious as the scent of garlic and cheese filtered into the entryway. "Anyone hungry?"

As they ate in the kitchen, Ella caught Autumn up to speed on the most recent events.

Autumn didn't comment much, but when Ella

finished, she asked, "Now will your mom finally get a new lock and a security system?"

"She's not in any position to argue now anyway," Ella conceded.

"We're installing a new system at Graceway tomorrow," Roman said.

"Good. This is getting out of control." Autumn fluffed her shiny hair and drummed mint-green fingernails on the table.

"Speaking of which, did you get my message? I'm working on a list of who had access to Graceway, and who may have had the key code," Ella said.

"Right. I got the message but haven't had a chance to give it much thought."

"That's okay," Ella responded. "I'm going to grab names from the visitor log, but if you have anyone to add, let me know."

"Sure. Send me the list when you're done and I'll take a look. Are you doing the same thing for people who had access to your mom's house?"

"Yeah. I'll send that one to you, too. It's pretty thorough, but you might think of someone else."

Autumn turned in her chair and kicked her cowgirl-booted feet up onto the counter, spearing Ella with an assessing look. "How have you been feeling?" she asked. "Because you look terrible."

If Ella was offended, she didn't show it. "I feel better than I look, I'm sure," she said with a laugh.

"Still taking your meds?"

"Yes, Mom," Ella said with sarcasm.

"Need me to pick up any refills on Monday? I've got a bunch of errands."

"I think I still have a few days left. I'll check and let you know."

"Are you always so popular?" Triss interrupted, calling out from the living room. "Looks like that pastor is back. And he's got someone with him. Younger guy."

Autumn suddenly swung her legs down from the countertop and stood. "I don't want to crowd the place," she said. "I'll go on home. Keep me posted."

"I will," Ella said, walking her to the door. "Thanks for the pizza."

Ahead of them Roman opened the door, chilly night air flooding in as Autumn walked out and the two men approached the house.

"That was a quick exit," Roman commented.

"She and Doug went on a few dates recently," Ella whispered. "He's a little clingy, apparently."

Roman couldn't quite imagine Autumn going on one date with Doug, let alone a few, so it was easy to see how the relationship hadn't worked out.

"We won't stay long," Pastor Wright said preemptively to Ella as he and his son walked up the porch steps.

Doug held out a store-bought loaf of iced pumpkin bread. "Dad told me you weren't up to visitors, but we wanted to make sure you were okay."

Roman caught the barely suppressed weariness in Ella's expression, but she stepped back to let the two men into the house. "I'll probably fade pretty fast, but come on in."

It didn't take long to determine that the pastor and Doug hadn't come for a social call. It was clear they wanted to assess Ella's mental state. The pastor had already voiced his concerns about her suicide attempts, and Doug obviously shared the pastor's sentiments. To add insult to injury, the root of their concerns centered around their church.

Anchor of Hope Fellowship regularly provided a major source of funding to Graceway and they needed to make sure someone competent was in charge while Ella's mom was ill. As they peppered Ella with pointed questions, she was tight-lipped in her answers.

The longer they talked, the brighter the fire blazed in her eyes. Roman was about to call an end to the visit when Ella's phone rang.

She glanced at the screen. "I should take this…"

The pastor stood and Doug joined him. "We've

probably overstayed our welcome anyway. Keep us posted?"

Ella nodded. "Thanks again for the visit," she said, answering the phone as the men made their way to the door.

Triss was already pulling it open, clearly ready for them to depart, as well. But Roman's attention fixed on Ella, her face stark white, her phone pressed tightly to her ear.

"Oh, no," she said, anguish in her voice.

He sent her a questioning look, but she held up a finger as she listened.

The pastor and Doug paused in the doorway, silence enveloping the room as they waited for the news.

"I'm so sorry, Almaz," Ella finally said, her troubled gaze catching Roman's. "Let me see what I can do on my end and I'll call you back as soon as I can."

Moments later she ended the call, her hand dropping to her side.

"There's been a fire at Graceway Village Ethiopia."

"What happened?" Doug asked, his face drawn in concern as he stepped back into the living room and Triss closed the door.

"They don't know," Ella answered. "They couldn't get it contained." Her eyes were bright with renewed energy and resolve, all signs of exhaustion masked by the fuel of the emergency at hand.

"Is anyone hurt?" the pastor asked.

"Everyone made it out unharmed, but the main center's a total loss and so are most of the tenant rooms."

"All those families will be displaced," Pastor Wright said, running his hand through his silver hair. "This is terrible."

"How many people are we talking about?" Roman asked.

"At last count, I think there were eight families," Ella said. "More than twenty children between them. Plus Graceway staff."

"Does Graceway have an emergency fund?" Roman asked, digging for a solution to the problem at hand.

"I don't know about an emergency fund," Ella said. "But the overseas fund should have enough money to put the families up in hotels for quite a while."

"That will work for the immediate, at least," the pastor said.

"But it's not a long-term solution," Ella said, straightening. "We could possibly pull funding from the other projects in Ethiopia until we figure out where we can put the families while we rebuild."

The pastor nodded. "That's a logical first step."

"We could also make an announcement at

church tomorrow," Doug suggested. "These families are going to need more than room and board, if everything was destroyed. We could take up a special collection."

"That would be really helpful," Ella said quietly, and the despair on her face tugged at Roman's heart. Despite the energy she had rallied, she looked downright exhausted and utterly alone.

"Could you take a few minutes at the end of the service tomorrow to talk to the congregation about what's happened and the specific needs?" the pastor asked. "Seeing as you're standing in for your mom, it would probably be best coming from you."

"Of course," Ella said. "I'll call Almaz back and tell her the plan." She moved to the door in a clear effort to usher the pastor and Doug out of the house.

"Would you be available for an emergency board meeting directly after service tomorrow?" the pastor asked. "We can hold it in one of our conference rooms."

"Sure, I'll be there," she responded.

"Great, we'll see you then," he said, stepping outside and pulling his sports coat tighter. "Strange weather," he commented as he waved a brief goodbye and hurried toward his car.

Doug stepped onto the porch and offered a hand to Roman. "Looks like you've got everything under control, but if you need anything at all, just let us know."

"Will do," Roman said.

"Take care, Ella," Doug said. "See you in the morning."

"Good night. Thanks for stopping in." She closed the door behind them and turned to Roman. "I'd better call Almaz," she said. "I can't even imagine how those families are feeling right now. There are newborn babies there, lots of young kids…" She was pacing back and forth in front of the couch now, her mind clearly reaching for solutions. "Those moms are probably worried they're going to end up right back on the streets and—"

"Slow down, Ell," Roman said, stepping in front of her. And before he could convince himself to back away, he slid his arms around her and tugged her close. It was a mistake, and he knew it. A six-year time gap was erased the moment her cheek came to rest against his chest, her hands warm on his back. "You're not doing this alone, remember?" And, for a moment, all the reasons they'd separated so long ago were lost on him. "I'm right here with you," he added, "and I'm not going anywhere."

NINE

Ella felt safe for the first time in weeks. Her head rested beneath Roman's chin, his heart beating a steady rhythm under her ear. This...this was right where she needed to be. He grounded her. He always had.

I've missed you, she thought. But she didn't dare say it.

And then he was loosening his embrace, stepping away. Putting space between them again.

"Don't let your mind jump ahead," he told her. "Call Almaz back. Find out what the immediate needs are. Ask if she has ideas on where the families could be put up. Find out what that will look like financially. We'll go from there."

"You're right," she said. "Let me go give her a call. Then I need to get working on what I'll say tomorrow."

"You do that. I'll work on my end. If you need to run anything by me, I'll just be out here."

"Thanks."

She detoured to the kitchen and quietly took the medicine she'd assured Autumn she was taking, realizing she would, in fact, need refills soon. On a whim, she snagged her prescription sleeping pills and hurried down the hall toward her room to make the phone call, propelled by Roman's encouragement and the lingering warmth of his embrace. But her chest felt tight as she picked up the phone. Back in Colorado, she was confident and decisive at her job. She knew the territory. Here, she was a fish out of water, trying to hang on to the organization her mom had built.

One step at a time. That's what her counselor would have reminded her. Focus on the first task at hand and don't get caught up looking too far ahead. She sent up a silent prayer and then dialed Almaz.

Hours later, Ella jerked awake, sitting up from where she must have fallen asleep at the small desk in her room. She looked at the clock. Just past ten. She could hear nothing but the low murmur of the television in the living room.

Strange that her mom was still up. She normally turned in by nine.

She stood and walked to her door, feeling strangely woozy. Nothing a good night's sleep wouldn't cure. Ignoring the all too familiar roil of nausea she'd been fighting regularly for the past couple of weeks, Ella headed down the hall to the living room, then stopped short.

Roman.

What was he doing sitting on the couch in her mom's living room? Her heart beat wildly, confusion swirling.

He wore khaki tactical pants and a black T-shirt, and was leaning over his laptop, his cell phone next to him on the couch. The television cast shadows on his face and when he glanced up, Ella's breath caught at the soft way he looked at her.

"Doing okay?" he asked.

She reached for an answer. He was sitting there as if he belonged. As if six years hadn't passed since they'd last seen each other. No, she wasn't doing okay.

"Ella?" He cocked his head to the side, his gaze assessing.

"Yeah," she managed to say. "I'm fine." Something was wrong. She was reaching for memories just at the edge of her conscience and something there kept her from revealing her confusion.

"You sure?" he asked, his eyes narrowing.

"Just tired, I think," she said. She needed to be alone, to figure out what was going on. She needed space. "I'm going to turn in."

She started back to her room, pulse racing, mind searching for information she couldn't seem to access.

"How'd the phone call go?" Roman asked.

Phone call? Ella considered the question, tried to make sense out of it. But she came up empty. "It went okay," she hedged as she continued down the hall. "I'll fill you in later."

She hurried back to her room, but Roman caught up with her. His hand came to her arm. "What's going on, Ell?" he asked. His breath was warm on her neck and a shiver ran down her spine.

She didn't turn to look at him. "Nothing," she said. "Just tired." She took a step forward into her room, but his grip on her arm remained firm.

"Tell me," he urged quietly. "Is Almaz okay? Did you get other news?"

Almaz. Ethiopia. The memories flooded back and her heart rate spiraled down in relief.

She turned to Roman, finally meeting his eyes. "It's late, Roman," she said, too weary to explain the memory lapse. "I'm sure you're just as tired as I am. You barely got a break today."

He shrugged. "I'm used to it. Why don't you sit for a few minutes and tell me about the call?" He gestured toward the living room, and Ella nodded, reluctantly following him.

He sat back on the couch and made room for her next to him, shifting a folder to the coffee table.

"Almaz seems to be handling the situation really well," she said, settling on the couch and stuffing a pillow behind her back. Her heart rate had started to settle, and she would just have to ignore the inviting scent of his cologne and the half cushion separating them on the couch. Because the only other alternative would be to scoot in close and curl up against his side. That's what she wanted to do more than anything—ever since he'd hugged her earlier and memories had sprung fresh, watering parts of her heart she'd neglected for too long.

"But it's tough," she continued, dismissing her wayward thoughts. "She's scrambling, reaching out to everyone she knows to make sure each family has shelter for the night. Of course, that's just a short-term solution. There are some guest-houses nearby that she said are pretty reasonable, and food's included."

"Any idea what the financial side will look like for Graceway?"

"I got an email from Wes. He forwarded me the latest account balances. There's an emergency reserve fund that should cover about a month of room and board for all the families."

"That'll buy you some time."

She nodded. "But I want a detailed look at the finances, and I feel like he's giving me the run-around."

"Someone else must have access to the ac-counts, right?" Roman asked.

"Jim Cannon. He's the treasurer on the board of directors. I'll talk to him after the meeting."

"Good call."

"In the meantime, I'm thinking if we hit pause on the two new Ethiopia projects for a while, we could divert those funds back to rebuilding the main center and supporting the families."

"Good plan. But you're frowning."

"A move like that will help the families in the immediate, but it will also put a lot of people out of jobs."

"The workers at the other sites couldn't come rebuild the new center?"

"The other sites are pretty remote. Transportation would be difficult."

"Sounds like a logistical nightmare," Roman commented.

"The chosen sites were deliberate," Ella explained. "Graceway could provide jobs and financial resources for some very poor and remote villages while also keeping single-mom families intact."

"I see the dilemma," Roman said. "Families were counting on that income."

"Right, and not only that, but there were families already on the waiting list for the program. Now their wait will be that much longer."

"All you can do is take one step at a time," he said. "Anchor is huge. They'll probably be able to donate some resources. And don't underestimate the special collection tomorrow. People tend to be generous where moms and kids are involved."

"Maybe. I just wish my mom could be there tomorrow. She'd probably be a lot more effective as a speaker. She has more invested."

"I don't know about that. You seem to have picked up right where you left off when you moved. You were there when Graceway opened and you helped your mom run it for several years."

"I was young and—"

"Don't sell yourself short. Graceway was a one-dimensional outreach program to help single moms find jobs before you suggested expanding the vision. Opening rooms for those moms and their kids gave them new hope, more opportunities."

"Ideas are easy. Implementing them—that takes resources, staff, thousands of hours... I always had the ideas, but wasn't around much to help get them off the ground."

Her attention turned to Isaac, who had curled up into a round little ball in her lap while she'd rubbed his head.

"Resources, staff, thousands of hours, true," Roman said. "But ideas...they stem from the heart. Your heart has been in this organization from the start. Even if you haven't been around much, I'd say your heart is as heavily invested as your mom's."

She sighed, unable to shake the sadness that had latched onto her since the phone call. "I know you're right. I just hope I say the right things so the congregation sees what we see."

"You need to remember that it's not all on you."

"Well, it kind of is. I mean—"

"No, Ella," he said, his tone warm and reassuring. "Yes, you've got a job to do. You've got to manage the problem in Ethiopia, and you've got to request funding for the emergency and figure out how the finances will work. But that's where your responsibility ends. You just do what's before you, one thing at a time, and make the best decisions you can with the information you have. God will take care of the rest."

She looked at him then, her hand resting on Isaac's back, eyes stinging with gathering tears.

"Will He?" she asked. "How do you know that, Roman? What if He doesn't? What if the money falls short? What if we have to close the program and those women and children end up on the streets? What if—"

"You'll drive yourself crazy with all those what-ifs. He has a plan for those moms and their kids, just like He has a plan for you, for your mom, for Graceway. It's not up to you."

Ella didn't say anything for a long moment and Roman's gaze skimmed over the short, red waves of hair framing her heart-shaped face, eyes blazing with worry. The scent of her shampoo swept between them and he wanted more than anything to pull her close again. It's what she probably needed more than any exchange of words. He shouldn't, though. The brief embrace they'd shared earlier had taken him back years, made him wonder if the time they'd spent apart really even mattered anymore. But then he recalled the day Shield had opened, when Ella hadn't bothered to show up. That action had spoken more clearly than any words—and it had told him that what they had shared could never be resurrected.

Tonight, though, none of that mattered. Tonight, they were simply old friends tossed back together by circumstance, and he would be there for her no matter what happened.

"What are you most afraid of?" he asked.

"That I'm not going to like His plan," she said in a near whisper.

Heartbreak and doubt seeped out of those shaky words, and he couldn't blame her.

"That's a possibility," he said. "But you don't have any control over that."

"That doesn't make me feel much better," she said with a wobbly smile.

"I won't tell you everything will be fine and it will all work out like a fairy tale," Roman said. "But the way I see it, you've got two choices— you can let worry paralyze you, or you can move forward and set your mind on hope."

She took a deep breath and released it, as if trying to rein in all the tentacles of worry. "I know you're right," she said reluctantly.

"Your job right now is to get some sleep for tomorrow. Do you want to run over what you plan to say first?"

"Not really. It's not my nerves that are getting to me."

"What is it?" he asked, suddenly aware of their closeness.

"The past couple of months…they've been overwhelming, that's all," she said, glancing away.

He knew she was trying to brush off the painful and steer away from another deep conversation, not appear like she was looking for sympathy.

"But I'll be okay," she said quickly. "You're right that I need some sleep." She started to stand, but he tugged on her hand to keep her there a moment longer.

"You're going to get through this," he told her. "I know it doesn't feel like it right now, but you will. You're one of the most determined people I've ever known."

The sweetest smile curved along her lips, but sadness still glistened in her eyes.

Whether it was the smile or the sadness that drew him to her, he didn't know, but Roman leaned close, pausing just short of her lips. Did she feel the current of attraction like he still did?

She closed her eyes and tilted her head a fraction of an inch, the only invitation he needed. His lips met hers tenderly at first. But when her arms slid over his shoulders, her soft sweater grazing his neck, her sweet scent enveloping him, he was lost for a moment.

Lost in memories. The gap closed, and no time had passed at all between their parting and their meeting again. Her taste was addictive and exhilarating. He wondered why he had ever let her go.

"Hunter says—oh!"

Triss's voice broke the kiss and they flew apart, both turning to see her at the end of the hallway.

"It can wait," she said and turned heel down the hall.

Ella's shoulders were shaking, her head down. Crying? He touched a hand to her arm. "Ella?"

She turned toward him, her hand over her mouth, laughter bubbling up.

He hadn't heard that laugh in so long.

"We surprised her, I think," she said breathlessly.

She had never looked more beautiful.

Or so off-limits.

Roman stood, walked over to the surveillance monitors for no other reason than to put space between him and Ella. Nothing had changed. Ella was still a client—a vulnerable client with her life at stake. And one kiss, one moment of weakness, did not change their current circumstances or erase the pain of the past.

His cell phone dinged and he checked the screen. "Looks like Triss has resorted to texting me from the kitchen," he said.

Ella laughed. "Anything important?"

"Just an update on our team that will be at the church tomorrow."

Ella nodded and walked to the windows to peek out at the snow. "Looks like it's slowing down," she said, as if they hadn't just shared a kiss that could melt every last snowflake.

No harm done, he told himself. They weren't teenagers anymore. They could recognize the kiss for what it had been—a momentary lapse in judgment sparked by memories of young love.

"We may get another inch or two after midnight," Roman said. The weather. A safe, mundane topic. "You turning in?"

"I probably should."

"Tomorrow, we'll want to head out early if you want to stop by Graceway on the way to church. Seven thirty okay?"

"Perfect," she said, moving away from the window.

"Try to get some sleep. And, Ella?"

She paused, looking back at him again.

"Let me know if you have any more of those memory lapses, okay?"

He caught the slightest hesitation before she nodded.

"Good night, Roman."

Roman was pretty sure she'd had one of her memory problems earlier. The look in her eyes had been blank and confused, but almost as soon as he'd keyed into the change, she had seemed to snap back to reality and he couldn't be sure he'd seen what he'd thought he'd seen. And what would her motive be for not admitting the problem?

A flicker of movement on the security monitors caught his attention. Roman pocketed his phone and crossed back to the monitors. The street was still and quiet out front, the backyard empty. The only disturbance in the snow out back was the narrow path Hunter had shoveled earlier for Isaac to do his business. Was his mind playing tricks on him? He'd been running on a dangerously low amount of sleep, after all...

His phone chimed and a text came in from Triss.

Heading out for a perimeter check.

Roman entered the kitchen and found Triss pulling a beanie onto her head.

"I'll do the rounds," he offered.

"I've got it," she said.

"It's freezing out there. Let me take care of it," he insisted, leaving the kitchen and returning to the foyer to retrieve his boots.

She followed at his heels. "I'm pretty sure I'm not in danger of getting trapped in a snowdrift or anything."

Roman laughed, turning back to her with his boots already on. She looked annoyed. "I didn't think you would," he said, grabbing his coat from the rack. He was trying to be a gentleman, truth be told, but he knew Triss well enough to predict she wouldn't take kindly to that admission. "I just need some air." The statement was true enough anyway. Being in the Camden home had triggered memories he hadn't entertained in a long time.

He stepped outside and his boots crunched salt on the concrete porch. He inhaled sharply at the brutal cold. The chill was almost enough to distance himself from all those memories. Almost.

Dim streetlights reflected the flurries, not a star in sight. The houses lining Midnight Lane were mostly dark. Enough snow had fallen to blanket the grass. The front yard was pristine, the covered sidewalk void of footprints.

Roman walked to the street, looking up and down but seeing nothing. Satisfied, he turned on his flashlight and headed around to the backyard. The newly installed floodlights cast a bright glow over the yard, leaving few shadows to be explored. Still, he walked the yard to be sure. He was turning back toward the house when he noticed something in his periphery.

He glanced at the back fence and moved closer. Snow capped the old picket fence in a straight line. Except for near the far right corner. There, where the light couldn't reach, the top of the fence was bare. Roman shone the flashlight up and down the fence line and along the ground, but saw nothing else unusual.

It could have been the wind. Or an animal.

But he didn't think so.

More likely it was someone peering over the fence from the opposite yard. He stepped up to the fence line and flashed his light into the yard on the other side.

Footprints.

They led from the side yard up to the fence line and all the way along the fences separating the two yards. Someone had been watching the Camden house.

Roman climbed over the fence and walked the yard, noting the footprints were fresh. He walked to the front of the house and peered up and down the street for any signs of a lurker.

Whoever had come must have noticed the security cameras in the front and decided to try a back way in. Roman would go back inside and check the surveillance footage. The camera may have picked up someone, even if he and Triss hadn't noticed any movement.

He jogged back to the house and let himself in. He kicked off his boots but didn't bother with his coat as he sat at the monitors and rolled the footage back.

"Find something?" Triss asked, appearing at his side.

"Afraid so," he said. But he had a feeling it wouldn't be enough to offer any useful clues. Within a few minutes, he discovered he was right.

"There he is," he said, pausing the screen and looking hard at the darkened corner of the fence line.

"Ten twenty-two," Triss said, reading the time stamp. "Just a few minutes ago."

It was easy to see how the creeper had almost gone unnoticed. He was wearing dark clothes, he'd barely raised his head above the fence line and he hadn't stuck around long.

Roman lightened the screen and increased the contrast, zooming into the corner and watching the clip again. The crouching figure came to a half stand at the corner of the yard, a gloved hand grasping the fence where the snow had been disturbed, the other hand holding a pair of what appeared to be night-vision goggles.

He'd watched the house, barely moving, for almost two minutes exactly. Then he'd ducked below the fence line and disappeared.

"That doesn't tell us a whole lot," Triss said.

"It tells us two things," Roman said. "We let this guy get too close and we need more light out back."

TEN

Almost as soon as Ella opened her eyes the next morning, she closed them again, her cheeks heating from the memory of the night before.

Oh, that kiss.

One touch of Roman's lips on hers had erased years of regret and loss.

But only for a moment.

Ella's heart sank. Almost as soon as Roman had stood from the couch, reality had flooded in.

She'd spent years wishing she could go back in time and make different decisions the night of Brooklyn's murder. Wishing she could tell herself not to leave campus that night, not to suggest a movie while waiting with Roman to walk his sister back to the dorms. One innocent idea had made the difference between life and death. Except that wasn't the only role Ella had played in Brooklyn's murder. If Roman knew the whole truth, he wouldn't want to be in the same room as Ella—let alone kiss her.

Ella flung her covers back and crossed the room to her closet. She paired black leggings and a high-necked lilac tunic sweater to hide the pinkish-blue bruise. She'd rather be warm than fashionable any day.

She arranged her hair with a few pins to cover the bald scar that was taking ages to heal. As she dug around in the closet for shoes, she smelled something savory and a little bit sweet. Voices and quiet laughter filtered down the hall. Ella finally slipped her feet into short black boots and followed the scent of breakfast and the sound of voices.

"Who's the chef?" she asked, turning into the kitchen.

Autumn was at the stove, flipping pancakes and frying up eggs, Isaac at her feet, hoping something might miss the pan. He seemed to be healing just fine, thankfully. The rest of the crew had gathered, as well—Luke, Roman, Triss and Hunter.

"Hey, sleepyhead," Autumn called, taking her eyes off the stove for a moment.

"It's like a party in here," Ella said.

"Shift change," Roman explained, flashing a smile.

She could barely make eye contact with him, emotion stirring deep.

"I just dropped in to cook you breakfast," Autumn said. "Good thing I brought plenty."

Behind her, Luke was rummaging through the fridge and pulled out a carton of orange juice and a bowl of grapes. "Morning," he said, setting the items on the table where Roman and Hunter were looking over something on Roman's laptop.

"Autumn cooked enough to feed a small army," Hunter said, motioning to the feast.

"It looks amazing." Ella poured herself a cup of juice, then crossed the kitchen and grabbed her pill bottles from the cabinet near the stove.

"Looks like you need refills, after all," Autumn said over her shoulder. "I can grab them this afternoon."

"That's okay. I'll call them in after church and pick them up at the drive-thru. But thanks."

"Sure," Autumn said, sliding a stack of pancakes onto a serving platter and adding it to the table. "Roman filled me in on what happened in Ethiopia." She shook her head. "It's just one thing after another around here. Sit down, have some food."

Conversation buzzed in the small kitchen, spreading a sense of warmth throughout the house. Ella had been doing this alone for weeks. Even though she was paying Roman's crew to be here, she was relieved to finally share the burden. For the first time in quite a while, she felt safe.

She'd always been independent, rarely accepting help and even more rarely asking for it. There was a lesson to be learned here, she knew—

sometimes sharing a burden was the only way to survive.

Triss scooted her chair back, her phone in hand. "I'm heading home, unless you need anything else."

"The rest of the day's covered," Roman said. "Thanks, and be careful on the roads."

"That would take away all the fun," she said with a rare grin, and waved goodbye as she let herself out.

"So, Roman told me you're stopping by Graceway on the way to church?" Autumn asked Ella.

Ella glanced at Roman and he nodded. "Tyler gave me the all clear. They wrapped up the scene late last night."

Autumn took a sip of juice and started buttering her pancake. "You know, I was thinking…" she said. "Your mom had a house key hanging at Graceway last year. It might still be there."

"What? Why?" Ella asked.

"When she first started chemo, she was in and out of the hospital a lot, and trying to coordinate someone to take care of Isaac was a problem. She figured it would be easiest to keep a key out for whoever needed it."

Ella caught Roman and Hunter exchanging a look. "What was she thinking?" Ella asked.

"She was thinking she could trust everyone at Graceway," Autumn said. "And it wasn't out in plain sight—not just anyone could see it and know it was a key to her house."

"Where was it? I'll check to see if it's still there."

"In the kitchen, attached to a little magnet on the side of the fridge," Autumn said, leaning down and handing Isaac some bits of bacon.

Ella scooped the dog up as he licked the grease off his tiny black nose. "This guy's enough of a butterball," she said. "No more bacon."

Autumn laughed and patted his head. "He sure is a cute little butterball," she said. "Poor thing with his paw. He must have been beside himself the other night."

"He was actually pretty lazy, snoozing on the couch while some psycho was hiding in the house," Ella said with an eye roll.

"He didn't even warn you?" Autumn asked. "I mean, he's never exactly been a ferocious guard dog, but doesn't he always bark at strangers?"

"Usually, yes." It wasn't the first time Ella had considered that whoever had been in the house the other night hadn't been a stranger to Isaac.

"He didn't bark at me," Roman pointed out. "But then again, it was late, he was injured, and isn't he pretty old?"

"He's around eleven, I think," Ella said. "He was a rescue when my mom adopted him. And you're right—he's not the most alert or aggressive."

"Some guard dog you are," Autumn said to Isaac while passing him a tidbit of egg.

Roman pushed back from the table. "Ella, as soon as you're ready, we can head to Graceway."

"Let me just help Autumn with the dishes. Ten minutes okay?"

"I'll help, too," he said.

"I've got it, you two," Autumn insisted, waving them away. "What's so important about going to Graceway so early anyway?"

Ella hesitated, realizing that once she told Autumn what she was looking for, the truth would come out about contacting TechSavvy. "I'm looking for a flash drive I misplaced," she said, hoping Autumn wouldn't ask more questions.

"What flash drive?"

Ella's heart sank. She should have known Autumn's curiosity would win out.

"I should have told you earlier," she said. "I hired a private company to see what else they could retrieve from our network and my mom's computer after the virus. What they found is on the drive."

Autumn's face fell, a mixture of hurt and anger darkening her eyes. She poured more syrup on her pancake before responding. "How much were they able to retrieve?"

"About sixty percent of the files. I'm sorry, I—"

"Don't apologize," Autumn cut in. "It's not

against the law to hire someone else. But, really, Ella, you could have talked to me about it first."

"I should have, you're right," Ella admitted, feeling like a rotten friend.

Autumn shrugged. "What's important is they were able to recover some of the files. Go ahead and get to your morning. I've got things covered here."

"You made a huge breakfast. The least I can do is—"

"I've got it," Autumn repeated. She seemed determined to have her way.

Ella hesitated, knowing that Autumn's pride was hurt, if not her feelings.

Roman caught Ella's attention and gestured toward the hall. "We'll get out of here, then," he said to Autumn. "You're an amazing cook," he added. "Thanks."

"Glad ya'll enjoyed it," Autumn responded, her tone just a little bit flat as she started clearing dishes from the table. "Be safe."

It was just after seven thirty when they pulled up to the curb in front of Graceway.

"Want me to come inside?" Luke asked Roman as he put the vehicle in park and unlocked the doors.

"Yeah, we'll do a sweep and then you can keep surveillance outside with Hunter," Roman answered. "Hunter, once Luke comes out, you can take up the back."

"Got it."

Ella followed Roman and Luke up the walkway, her head down against the biting wind. Inside, her gaze traveled up to the catwalk, a shudder rippling over her at the memory of last night.

"We'll clear the area before we get started," Roman said, pulling his gun from its holster. "Follow us, but stay back a few feet."

The old building seemed especially quiet, a chill in the air. Ella followed the men as they started a methodical search of the first floor. They worked seamlessly together, barely a word between them. At the front desk, Ella opened the top drawer and grabbed the visitor log before catching up to the guys as they entered the kitchen. She easily spotted the key Autumn had told them about. "Key's still here," she said.

"Who knows how many people used it, or who may have copied it," Roman said, sobering her small victory. He and Luke swept through the small kitchen and the three cubicles behind it, opening closet doors and cabinets as they walked.

A door creaked open from the back of the building, and Ella froze. Roman swung around, positioning himself in front of her, gun at the ready.

He motioned underneath the desk of a nearby cubicle and Ella ducked down and folded herself into the space. She clasped her arms around her knees, motionless except for the tremor in her hands and the frantic beat of her heart. She strained to hear beyond the cubicle and her own heartbeat. She could no longer see Roman or Luke, but knew they had crouched behind a half wall and split in separate directions.

She should call for help. Getting to her phone without making noise would be next to impossible, but she had to try. Slowly, she shifted her legs to the side, reaching silently for her purse.

"Hello?" a man's voice called out. "Is someone here?"

She knew that voice. Ella exhaled a sigh of relief and crawled out from under the desk, standing just as JT appeared at the door to Marilynn's office.

"Whoa!" he said, backing away from Roman and Luke, his arms coming up in defense.

Roman lowered his gun and nodded to Luke, who did the same.

"Sorry, JT," Ella said, her pulse coming back down. "I needed to grab a few things from the office and after what happened yesterday, we can't be too careful."

JT frowned, eyeing the armed men. "I heard about it," he said to Ella. "Glad you're okay."

"Thanks. Surprised to see you here on a Sunday."

His frown deepened, his eyes glossy. Had he

been crying? "I've been a bit behind lately. Had a few things I wanted to get done before tomorrow," he said. "Didn't expect anyone to be here, least of all anyone with a gun."

She noticed that Roman didn't offer an apology.

"I was about to head home. Haven't been here long, but I can't concentrate anyway," JT continued. He sighed heavily. "Can't understand about Marilynn…" His voice broke, pink rising along his neck. "How someone could do that to a woman like her…"

Ella stepped closer and put a hand on his arm. "I know, JT. I'm so sorry. I know you two were close."

He cleared his throat and turned away. "Thank you," he said. "I'd better get on." He made his way to the front door and let himself out.

Ella knew JT and Marilynn had gotten along well, and she had long suspected he was interested in pursuing a relationship. But he was a reserved guy, old-fashioned, and a long-time bachelor. She'd had no idea how deeply his feelings had run.

Roman locked up after JT and took his time looking around. He motioned to Marilynn's office. "What else do you know about JT?" he asked, opening the door and flipping on a light as he stepped inside.

"He's worked here since we broke ground,"

Ella said. "He's a really sweet guy. No idea why he was in Marilynn's office, though."

The office was endlessly organized and smelled of Marilynn's sweet floral perfume.

"Notice anything wrong?" Roman asked.

"No." Except that Marilynn wouldn't be coming back. Ella's eyes stung, pressing away the images that rose up in her imagination of what those last moments had been like for one of the kindest women Ella had ever met. Marilynn and her mom had been friends for decades. Her mother would be devastated—if she ever regained consciousness.

"Let's keep going, then." Roman flipped off the light and shut the door behind them. He and Luke made quick work of the second and third floors before Roman holstered his gun.

"I'll head outside," Luke said. "Got a key so I can lock up behind me?"

Ella handed him her keys and thanked him as he headed down the stairs.

"Looks like we're alone," Roman said, obviously referring to the fact that no one was lurking in the shadows, but Ella's breath caught at a memory long tucked away.

A snowy afternoon, a spontaneous movie date. The previews already rolling as they strode in, Roman's arm looped around her back, a box of popcorn in his other hand.

Not another soul in the theater.

"Looks like we're alone," he said with a wink.

"Maybe the movie's a dud," she responded.

"Or no one else was crazy enough to drive to the movies with this storm brewing," he said, leading the way to dead-center seats.

They settled in next to each other, Ella's cheek resting against Roman's shoulder, popcorn between them.

"Ready to get started?"

Roman's question pulled her out of the memory, and Ella refocused on him. He was standing in the doorway of her mom's office, a question in his gaze.

"Sure," she said, and followed him.

Someone had gotten rid of the ladder. And the noose. The desk had been moved back into place. Ella set down the visitor log and turned on the computer, sifting through the contents of the desk as it booted up. If she'd left the flash drive at Graceway, it'd be in her mom's office. She didn't see it anywhere.

"I think it's gone," she said, resigned. "Let me just see if maybe I already loaded the files onto this computer."

He was standing behind her, the warmth of his presence cocooning her in the chilly office. "That's the first order of business," he agreed. "Hopefully tomorrow we can take a look at the files TechSavvy recovered. Have you gotten any memories back?"

"No," she answered. "I have flashes of memory. Late nights in the office, looking through files. There's something… I just can't put my finger on what it is."

"You mean you think you had found something?"

She nodded, frustrated as she realized the computer didn't hold any clues. She shut it down and looked up at Roman. "It's just a sense I have. Maybe I just want to remember so badly, my mind is making things up."

"Somehow I doubt that," Roman said.

Ella slung her purse over her shoulder and stood. "Whatever's going on, it looks like we'll have to wait until tomorrow for—"

A beeping noise came from across the hall and they both swiveled around toward the open door. But the noise abruptly stopped.

Roman drew his gun. "You have your cell phone?"

"Yes."

"Stay here. I'm going to—"

A loud boom burst through the silence.

Ella gasped, instinct sending her to the floor as a bright spark exploded across the hall, accompanied by an ear-splitting crack that shook the building. Roman dropped down next to her, shielding her body with his.

"What was that?" she yelled, but the fire alarms

were blaring, and she knew. She knew exactly what it was.

"Stay close," Roman said, tugging on her hand and pulling her up and toward the door.

"The fire escape—" Ella started to say, but a blast of thick black smoke billowed into the office.

Roman reared back and Ella moved with him as flames shot across the hall outside the office. Flames that blocked their only way of escape. Roman shut the door, but smoke seeped under it, flames licking at the old wood. A perfect fuel for the fire.

"Quick, to the window!" Roman barked.

He grabbed her hand and tugged her across the office, then shoved open the window and pushed out the screen. Behind them, the flames began to claw their way along the front wall of her mom's office.

Roman pulled her to the windowsill and Ella sucked in cold, fresh air even as smoke and fire gathered behind them. Strong arms latched tightly around her, Roman's body shielding her from the scorching heat. Even the winter wind was no match for the thick smoke enveloping them.

Ella choked back a cough, terror setting in as she looked down.

She already knew what she'd see. She'd taken in the view of the water nearly every day since she'd come home. It was serene, idyllic. And, three stories up, a fire at their backs, it was a death trap.

ELEVEN

Distant sirens wailed toward the building, but Ella was sure they wouldn't make it in time. She leaned farther out the window, Roman's harsh breath near her ear, his arms around her middle.

Below, the grass was white with last night's snow, onlookers gathering across the street, watching in frozen horror. Where was Hunter? He would have been in the back. No sign of him, not that he could do much to help anyway. And what about Luke? He should have heard the explosion and come running.

"We might have to jump," she said, knowing it could be a death sentence. Or they could get away with a few broken bones or just some minor scrapes. They might be forced to take the chance.

"We wait until the last possible second." Roman's voice was hoarse, painful coughs punctuating each word.

Smoke enveloped them, pluming out the window. Ella dragged in a breath, coughing so hard her stomach hurt, tears streaking down her face. She tried to look back, gauge how close the fire was. Roman held her fast.

She squeezed her eyes shut against the stinging smoke. And she prayed.

"Don't cry," Roman whispered. "Help's coming."

She wiped her cheeks, moisture and soot coming away on her hands.

"Roman, I—" What? Have loved you since forever? Wish we could have another chance? Don't want to die?

"Look!" Roman yelled over her head.

Ella's attention swiveled to the yard below. Luke and Hunter were racing down the sidewalk, a huge ladder balanced on their shoulders. Despite their expert maneuvering along the snowy yard, Ella thought they'd never make it in time.

But then the onlookers moved into action. A man with a red hat ran to the ladder and took up the middle, and soon others followed, the ladder racing toward the building.

Bracing herself in the windowsill, Ella turned her neck, heat radiating behind her. Roman blocked her view. "Don't look back," he said. "We're almost out of here."

She knew he was protecting her, trying to keep her calm. Her biggest fear wasn't for her own life but for his. He'd die protecting her, she knew he would.

As Luke and Hunter led the strangers below to the building and the ladder cranked up just short of the window, she prayed like she hadn't prayed in years.

"Now!" Roman urged, helping turn her body so she could drop over the ledge. She clutched the windowsill, her feet searching for the rung of the ladder. Her chest hurt, her limbs heavy and slow. She felt a hand at her ankle.

"I'm right here!" Luke called, guiding her foot to the first rung and making sure she was securely positioned.

Quickly, they both started their descent, but Roman didn't follow. Above the ladder, he straddled the windowsill, flames fanning around him. He was waiting for her to get to safety. Black smoke filled the air, making it hard to see him as the ladder rattled under Luke and Ella's hurried descent. When her feet finally hit the ground, a numb shock set in.

Around her, everything seemed to move in slow motion at an echoing distance. The fire engine pulled up to the curb and firefighters raced toward the building. An ambulance arrived, paramedics filing out. Good Samaritans banged on the doors of nearby town houses and shouted for families to evacuate.

Ella doubled over, coughing uncontrollably until someone slipped an oxygen mask on her face and tried to lead her away from the building. She stood rooted to her spot, her gaze fixed on the ladder, her eyes burning and blurring. All she saw was smoke, and a desperate, painful fear took root.

She ripped off the oxygen mask and charged to the ladder. "Roman!" she yelled, her voice gritty and thick. Hands settled on her shoulders, urging her away from the smoke. "There's someone still up there!" she screamed, yanking away from the firefighters.

More hands joined in, tugging her away from the scene, but she wouldn't budge. He couldn't be gone. Only seconds ago, he'd been partway out the window. Had the smoke overcome him? She dragged in a painful breath, a sob lodged in her aching throat.

And then the soles of his black boots appeared, and Ella's heart jerked. He stepped off the ladder and pulled her into his arms.

"I'm right here," he said, his voice like gravel. Then he hooked an arm around her waist and led her away from the burning building. His chest heaved with suppressed coughs as they were both led to separate ambulances.

A blanket was draped over Ella's shoulders, an oxygen mask secured, and she was settled in the ambulance, watching Roman receive identical treatment just yards away.

He'd protected her up until the last seconds. Risked his life for hers. Their eyes met and he stood, wresting away from the paramedic who encouraged him to sit. His clothes and face dark with soot, he pulled his oxygen mask down as he closed the distance between them. Reaching a hand toward her, he tenderly pushed her hair from her eyes. "Remember this day the next time you doubt," he said, his voice sandpaper-rough. "You're never alone. God still answers prayers."

This time, Ella thought, a river of cynicism coursing through her veins. *This one time.* Why? Had she prayed harder? Concentrated more? Had more faith? More terror?

She thought about Brooklyn's death, about the year her friend had suffered in an abusive relationship, and about the months that followed. How Brooklyn's ex had stalked her and made her life miserable until he had finally found his opportunity. How much had Roman's family tried to protect her? How often had they prayed for her?

"We need to get going, sir." A paramedic appeared at Roman's side, interrupting Ella's thoughts. "Ready?"

Roman squeezed Ella's hand and let a paramedic settle the oxygen mask back on his face. His chest burned. So did his back. He didn't care. Ella was safe. That had been too close a call.

Someone was tending to his bare back, and the pain struck him then, strong and blistering and intense. He inhaled sharply, watching the building burn. There was no doubt in his mind the explosion had been caused by some sort of bomb. But how had it gotten there? Had someone been watching, climbing the fire escape during the small window of opportunity when no one was guarding the back? Or had the bomb been planted and either set on a timer or controlled through a remote?

"Everyone okay, Boss?" Triss asked, appearing suddenly at Roman's side. "Luke called me."

"Yes," he answered. "Thanks for coming. We'll need extra hands at the hospital."

Roman caught sight of Ella's ambulance as the paramedics prepared to pull out. "I need to go with her."

"I'll go with Ella," Triss said. "Luke's following the ambulance. We'll take care of her. Looks like you'll need some treatment."

"I'll be okay," he said through the mask. "Just need to catch my breath."

"Roman, your back's a mess," Triss said.

He knew she was right. The cold wind wasn't enough to numb the pain searing up and down his bare skin as the paramedics prepared him for transport.

He nodded, resigned. He'd have to trust his team for a while and get the burns taken care of or he wouldn't be good for much.

"All right, but don't let her out of your sight," he said. Mentally, he ran through a list of his weekend on-call employees. "Get Connor and Bryan up to the hospital, too, would you?"

"Already done," Triss said, ducking into Ella's ambulance.

He didn't like the idea of Ella going anywhere without him. It wasn't that he didn't trust his team. It was simply that whoever was after Ella was tenacious, his attempts growing bolder. There was no way to predict what he would try next.

For a few minutes back there, things hadn't looked good. The thought of losing Ella had dredged up every memory he had of her—and reminded him of what it had felt like to lose her years ago. He wouldn't fool himself into believing she was back in his life to stay, but he couldn't stomach the idea of anything happening to her.

He was an optimist by nature, but he'd be the first to admit that he and Ella had nearly died today. It was only by the grace of God that they'd made it.

Roman gritted his teeth as the paramedics continued to prep him for transport. The raw burns on his back were icy-hot, and his lungs were still on fire. A large group of onlookers had gathered and he wondered if the perpetrator was in their midst keeping watch.

It seemed he was becoming more reckless, as if he had a deadline. The attacks had escalated. The perp was no longer trying to disguise his actions as a suicide or an accidental hit-and-run. Why the change? Why the seeming franticness of action in comparison to the planned attacks? Could there be two perpetrators? Or only one, who was getting very desperate? And what could possibly be the motive? The sooner Roman could get bandaged up, the sooner he could get back to finding answers.

The emergency room was quiet early on a Sunday morning, and Roman was taken to a room immediately. Over the course of a couple of hours he was diagnosed with first-and second-degree burns on his back, the burns cleaned and dressed, and a dose of painkiller administered. He'd been receiving regular updates from Triss on Ella, who had been treated for minor smoke inhalation and released, opting to visit her mother for a while until Roman was finished with his treatment.

Roman checked out and had just left a message for Tyler when his phone vibrated with a text from Triss.

Mrs. Camden's awake. Floor 8, room 841.

Roman rushed to the elevators. He'd suspected that something fishy had happened with Mrs. Camden's car accident, and maybe now they could get more details.

The elevator climbed in slow motion and finally opened onto the eighth floor where Luke waited to greet him.

"We've got people at all the points of entry to this floor," he told Roman. "Mrs. Camden's that way." He pointed to his right.

Roman found the room quickly. The door was ajar and animated voices came from within. He tapped the edge of the door and poked his head inside.

"Come in," Ella said from her mom's bedside. Tears streamed down her cheeks, her hair in disarray. She still had traces of soot on her neck, but she was smiling and very much alive.

Julia Camden was sitting up in the bed, her face pale, her body frail. Her eyes looked dull and he wondered if she'd sustained a brain injury. A nurse was checking vitals as a doctor slipped past Roman and out of the room.

"Roman," Ella's mom said, her voice rough and quiet. "It's been a long time. And am I ever glad to see you now." Her lower lip trembled.

Roman scooted by Triss at the doorway and approached the bedside. "I'm here for whatever you need," he told Ella's mom, setting a hand over hers.

"She remembers the car wreck," Ella said. "And she says it wasn't an accident."

"Tell me what you remember," Roman said.

"Someone was following me home," Julia answered. "It looked like an SUV I'd seen earlier in the week. Navy blue or black with tinted windows. He'd tailed me close and made me nervous. But that night, he got right on my bumper—" Her voice broke and Ella rubbed her arm, passing her a tissue.

"Take your time," Roman said.

"All of a sudden, he came up on my left on a two-lane road. I thought he must be in some kind of a hurry, so I slowed down and let him pass. But after passing me, he sped up…and then pulled a fast U-turn and headed right back in my direction. It all happened so fast. The last thing I remember is slamming on my brakes and steering away from him."

"He forced you off the road," Roman said.

She nodded. "Yes."

"You said you'd seen the car earlier in the week. Do you think it was following you then? Any idea why you might be a target?"

"I don't know," she said, but she looked uncertain, as if she were searching for a memory just beyond reach.

Ella sat close to her mother, her hand never leaving her mom's arm. He saw her then for the woman she had become—the adult daughter stepping in to care for her mom's business, the competent doctor, the empathetic friend. All the qualities he'd fallen in love with had deepened and flourished, and he was filled with pride, which made no sense. He hadn't had anything to do with her in years, but he still felt interconnected with her life, with who she had been and who she had become.

A knock sounded at the door and Triss poked her head in. "Back to the house after this? Or are we still trying to make it to church?" she asked.

"Ella?" Roman asked.

She sighed. "Second service is about to start already, but I should try to go to the board meeting. It's really the last thing I want to do, but I know I should." She stood. "Can you swing me by the house so I can change and wash up real quick?"

"No problem," Triss said just as Officer Goodson appeared behind her in the doorway.

Ella invited him in, introduced him to her mother, then leaned down and pressed a kiss to her forehead.

"Ella, wait," her mom said, her expression troubled. "I have a bad feeling about something."

"What is it, Mom?"

"Graceway," she said. "I remember spending a lot of time looking over the bank accounts before the accident. I was worried that night, when I was driving. I don't know why but...can you try to look into it for me?"

"I've been trying, Mom, but Wes hasn't been reliable, and I don't have access to Graceway's bank accounts. I'm going to see Jim Cannon this afternoon."

"Here, let me give you the user name and password so you can get onto the account yourself."

Ella handed her phone to her mother, an empty memo open for her to key in the info.

"I wonder if you could have the bank freeze some of Graceway's assets while we're looking into this," Ella said.

"If you can get me my cell phone, I'll call tomorrow and find out," her mother said. "There's our account in Ethiopia, as well."

Ella moved over to the window where her sister had placed a small carry-on of their mother's belongings. "Here it is," she said, pulling out the phone and charger. "I'll set it to charge for you." She plugged it in and turned back to her mom. "We need to get out of here, but we'll come back to visit soon. You're in good hands. Roman's got a lot of people here looking out for you."

Roman nodded. "And we'll be adding security detail for you back at your home, as well, until this is resolved."

"Oh, I appreciate that so much, Roman, but I can't afford—"

"Money's off the table," he cut in gently. "You're practically family. I'm going to make sure nothing happens to you."

"We *were* practically family," Julia said, her expression sad. Her gaze passed between Roman and Ella, but she said nothing more. "Well, I accept and appreciate your help. Thank you."

Mrs. Camden's words haunted Roman all the way to the waiting car.

Practically family.

She was right. They *had* been.

He remembered evening block parties in the summer, catching lightning bugs in the spring, playing freeze tag with all the neighborhood kids. After he and Ella had started dating, they were almost never apart for dinner—eating together at one of their parents' houses. They'd pitch in and clean up afterward, then sit around watching television and sharing laughs and easy conversation.

Brooklyn's murder had slashed right through the peaceful comradery, destroying dreamy hopes of marriage and a couple of kids and walking hand in hand until they were old and gray.

All because Ella had innocently suggested they grab a movie while Brooklyn was in class.

"I knew we should have stayed on campus..." Roman said, his voice trailing off at the fresh gloss of sadness in Ella's eyes.

"I'm so sorry," Ella responded, her hand slipping over his, her voice breaking.

Her apology hung in the air as he silently replayed the previous night's conversation. He'd told her he wasn't sure about leaving campus. She'd shrugged off his concerns. He'd caved to her suggestion. Now his sister was dead.

Roman pulled his hand from hers and turned

away. "I need to get home," he said, and he got in his car and drove away.

The whirring of a Life Flight helicopter began overhead, and Roman's mind shifted to the present as the wind kicked up and he guided Ella to the open door of Triss's car. Ella slid into her seat and Roman followed, regret twisting fresh in his gut as he pushed the past aside and focused on the moment at hand.

Within an hour, the Shield team was set up at the church, and Roman held out his hand to Ella as she exited the car. "I'm thinking we don't let anyone know just yet that your mom's awake," Roman whispered as they walked toward the entrance of the church.

She nodded, her eyes serious. "Agreed," she said then glanced at her watch. "We're early."

"Looks like we'll catch the tail end of the service," Roman said as he surveyed the quiet parking lot. The pain meds were wearing off, but he wouldn't take any more. He needed to be at his best, and he was already feeling less alert than usual. Despite his doctor's orders to rest, however, he didn't see that happening any time soon.

Not with Ella's life on a very thin line.

TWELVE

Roman opened the door and followed Ella inside. He and his family still attended the same little church downtown and had never ventured further. Since jumping into Ella's case, however, Roman had spent a significant amount of time learning about Anchor of Hope Fellowship and its ties to Graceway.

It was no wonder Graceway was able to secure so much funding through the church's patrons. According to the most recent annual report, the nonprofit pulled in nearly eight million in revenue last year, almost a third of the funding funneling in through the church's contributions. That was a lot of money. But the program expenses accounted for more than eighty percent of the revenue and it sounded like Julia Camden had been struggling to keep up with the programs since her cancer diagnosis last year.

A thriving organization whose leader was

out of commission was ripe ground for greed and temptation.

Then Ella enters the picture. Smart, driven, organized Ella, with her big heart and her overarching sense of responsibility, had started putting Graceway back in order. And she'd started asking questions. But someone didn't want her to discover the answers.

"Let's just sit out here until the service is over," Ella suggested, pointing to a bar-height round table in what appeared to be an actual coffee shop in the middle of the church lobby.

She filled a cup of water on the way to the table. Roman pulled a stool out for her and took a seat across from her, his attention following hers to the large screen on the opposite wall. The lights were dim as Pastor Wright preached passionately from his pulpit.

Then the camera panned the congregation and Roman scanned the sanctuary, looking for familiar faces. Ella had told him that most of the staff at Graceway attended the church. Could someone under this roof be hunting her?

The police investigation was well under way, but that could take days, weeks, more. They didn't have the luxury of time. Roman's gaze dropped to Ella's profile. She'd carefully twisted her hair to the side and clipped it in place, strategically placing a scarf at her neck that almost hid the bruises.

Every day that passed, her attacker seemed to

be getting closer, but he'd have to get through Roman and his team first. Because no matter how desperate this lunatic might be to see Ella dead, it could never compare to Roman's desperation to make sure she lived.

Minutes passed as Ella tried to keep her mind on the sermon. But she was exhausted and pre-occupied by the man at her side—the reason why she had never been able to commit to another re-lationship. Every date had paled in comparison to the fiery chemistry and easy friendship she'd shared with Roman.

The draw she felt toward him hadn't melted away over the years like she'd convinced herself to believe. She'd run away with her grief and her guilty conscience, and she'd distanced her-self from what they'd shared. But nothing had changed.

She stole a glance at his hard profile, caught the way his attention fixated on the audience on-screen.

No, she was wrong. *Everything* had changed.

They weren't the same people they had been in their early twenties, before Brooklyn's death had ripped their world apart. She pined for what had once been, grieved for it, but knew that even if they could try again, give their relationship another chance, it would never be the same. Not unless she could tell him the whole truth and he could forgive her for it.

She shoved the idea aside and trained her focus on the screen, attempting to follow what the pastor was preaching. It was a story she'd heard a hundred times since she was a little girl. The woman who had been bleeding for years came and touched Jesus's robe and was healed.

Pastor Wright told the story with charisma, most of the congregation glued to his position at the pulpit.

Familiar and unwelcome cynicism rose up like bile. The woman had reached out and touched the robe in complete faith—and she'd been healed.

What did that say about Brooklyn's struggle for breath as her murderer strangled all the oxygen from her body? Marilynn's life of faith that ended so brutally? What of *their* faith? What of *their* healing?

Of course, the pastor didn't address that. Why would he? He was the most successful pastor on the East Coast. The only hard times he'd ever fallen into involved his wayward son, who'd turned his life around and come back to the fold just one short year after a lengthy prison sentence. An answered prayer. The prodigal son returning, just like the Bible stories. No, Pastor Wright didn't have experience with loss and lasting grief. He couldn't relate to the painful confusion and disappointment of prayers unanswered.

Shame immediately washed over her at the turn of her thoughts. As if she wished heartache on him. She didn't. Didn't wish it on anyone. Not to mention—this morning's escape from the fire and her mother's emergence from a coma had certainly put Ella in a place of humility and gratefulness. But life often didn't make sense and for every answered prayer, plenty more seemed to go unanswered.

"Doing okay?" Roman asked.

"I'll be fine," she said, touched by the compassion in his eyes. It was that compassion that had always drawn her to him. He saw struggles behind smiles, noticed people who needed help and were too proud or afraid to ask, and he stepped in wherever he could find a way to help.

His hand settled on her knee briefly, a warm assurance that he knew she was going through a lot. She ached to cover his hand with hers, to anchor herself to the steadiness he'd always offered.

But his hand slipped away and she realized belatedly the pastor had begun the closing prayer. Dutifully, she bowed her head, but she felt nothing. She hadn't felt anything in years when she prayed. So she had mostly stopped.

The prayer came to an end and church members began to file out of the sanctuary. The lobby filled with conversation and laughter, music flowing in from the worship center. Ella's pulse tripped, a flash of anxiety tempting her to flee the sudden crowd.

"We're so glad you're okay," someone said next to her.

Ella turned, meeting the kind eyes of an impeccably dressed man with dark gray hair and a clean-shaved face. She couldn't place who he was, but he looked familiar.

"Thank you," she responded.

"And Julia?" he asked. "Any change?"

Jim Cannon. The name came to her suddenly, his face clicking into place in her mind. He used to be the accountant at Graceway and had taken a job at the church last year. How had she forgotten? Worry edged in. Not her memory again, she hoped.

"We're just taking a day at a time," she responded vaguely.

Pastor Wright was approaching from across the lobby. "Ella, I'm so sorry about the fire this morning," he said. "If you need to miss today's meeting, we can certainly reschedule."

She heard his words but the meaning didn't register. Fear struck hard and sharp, and Ella froze, her mind suddenly blank and reaching. It was happening again. She looked at Roman and he cocked his head to the side, stepping closer, as if sensing she needed help.

"Thank you," Ella said, her heart clamoring,

hands shaky. She stared at the pastor and Jim, not sure what they expected her to say.

"You all right, Ell?" Roman asked quietly in her ear.

She nodded, but started to turn away from the small circle. She needed space to calm down, to remember.

"I think everyone's here, if we want to head to the conference room."

Ella glanced up sharply to find Doug at her side.

She blinked, the memories flooding back. Right. The fire in Ethiopia. Her heart rate spiraled down, her breathing more controlled. Okay. She was okay.

For now, at least.

"Well, I'm happy to report that the donations have been pouring in all morning," Doug said to the group of board members gathered around the conference room table. "We're already at twenty-three thousand dollars—and that's just from the first service. Second service donations are being tallied."

"That's incredible," Ella said.

"I tried to contact Wes so he could present the current financials," the pastor said. "But I wasn't able to get hold of him."

"I haven't been able to, either," Ella said. "And he's been a no-show for the past week."

"That's not like him," Doug said. "I'll see if I can track him down tonight."

Roman made a mental note to do his own investigating immediately after the meeting. Wes, Graceway's accountant, could very well be involved in whatever was going on at the nonprofit. At the very least, locating him would rule out the possibility that there had been another victim.

"Let me know what you find," Ella said to Doug. "In the meantime, Jim, would you be able to help me if I have any financial questions?" Ella asked. "I'll be taking a detailed look at the accounts over the next few days."

"Sure," he replied.

"The most immediate problems we need to handle are how to continue operations here and how to house the families in Ethiopia during the rebuilding," Ella continued.

"I've got several ideas for our next steps," Pastor Wright piped in before Ella could say more. He pulled out a manila folder and began distributing stapled packets to each board member.

Roman listened carefully to the pastor's suggestions, impressed by his organization and business sense. The pastor proposed that Graceway Annapolis staff work out of the church offices during the rebuild, and there would be a temporary hold on construction at the satellite villages in Ethiopia. The funds for those projects would be reallocated to the Addis Ababa village as the restoration process was followed through.

The meeting ran smoothly until the discussion turned to sending a team to Ethiopia to help with immediate concerns. On this issue, it seemed, the entire room was divided.

The pastor and his son seemed adamant that they wait a week, as Doug was already scheduled to head the next missions group visit, departing Saturday. This would give them more time to prepare and gather resources. Other board members thought going sooner made more sense, and several volunteered their time.

Ella mentioned her already planned trip. Roman opened his mouth to disagree, but Doug beat him to it. "You've been through enough," he said.

"And your mom needs you," another added. Voices piped in their dissent and Ella sighed. No one could agree, and the hour was growing closer to two. Ella looked drawn and pale, and Roman decided it was time to step in.

"I suggest we table this conversation for a couple days. We'll postpone Ella's trip for now and revisit this conversation with a conference call in a day or two, after we get a clear picture of what the overseas needs are."

He didn't miss the annoyance that flashed over Ella's expression, but he wouldn't apologize for his executive decision. No way was she getting on a plane to Ethiopia tomorrow. The meeting was adjourned in quick succession and Roman opened the door to let Ella pass through.

Doug sidled up next to them as they walked toward the lobby. "Ella, thanks for being here," he said. "Your mom will be proud when she sees how you've been handling everything."

"Thanks, Doug. That means a lot."

His expression darkened to one of concern and his voice lowered. "That said, I really urge you to stay here. I know you feel connected to Graceway and you feel it's your responsibility, but a lot of us are emotionally vested in the program, too. An entire team of us are scheduled to leave at the end of the week, and we can keep in close contact with you."

"I appreciate that, Doug," she said. "I'll think about it and be in touch."

"Sure thing," he said with a kind smile, and excused himself.

"He's right, you know," Roman said as they walked out of the church into the cold afternoon. "I heard a lot of volunteers clamoring to go. Several were willing to get on a plane tonight."

"It makes sense for me to use the ticket I already bought," she said.

"You can reschedule for later and not lose the money, right?"

"I guess," she hedged. "But I don't know who I can trust to go in my place."

"Well, you can trust my team," Roman suggested. "I can get a couple guys on a plane within two days. You just give the instructions and they'll do any investigating you want done. It'll be safer that way."

He opened the passenger door for her, several other Shield vehicles turning their engines over as Ella got in, yanking on her seat belt with a little too much force.

"You seem frustrated," he commented, leaning over the door.

"I am."

"Why?"

"Because your suggestion makes a lot of sense and I know you're right."

He laughed and shut the door, climbing into the front passenger seat. "I'll make the arrangements tonight. Before we head back, I was thinking about stopping off at Wes Bentley's place. If he's avoiding you, we need to find out why. And if he's missing…"

"You think he could be another victim?" she asked, skepticism on her face.

"It's a possibility," he pointed out.

"I think he's just avoiding me," Ella told him. "He doesn't seem very reliable to me, but we need to try to find him, regardless."

"I wouldn't mind talking to Jim more in-depth later, either," Roman said. "What do we know about him?"

"He worked at Graceway for years," Ella noted. "Has a big family. Four or five teenage daughters and two sons—I think they're married with kids by now. He left last year to take the position at the church."

"Interesting. I'd like to know why."

"I never really gave it much thought," Ella said. "I'm sure the church position paid more. Wouldn't anyone take a step up like that?"

Probably. But Roman would still like to talk to the guy.

It didn't take long to drive the few miles to Wes's apartment. He lived in the basement apartment of a row house near downtown Annapolis.

"Looks like the entrance is in the back," Roman said, motioning for Ella to follow him along the salted walkway. Luke trailed close behind. They made their way around a square of winter-brown grass and approached the bright red door. Roman rang the doorbell, but when he didn't hear a chime, he rapped loudly on the door three times.

Beside him, Ella stood expectantly, her hands shoved deep into her coat pockets for warmth. He waited several moments before knocking again. Still, no answer.

"Now what?" Ella asked, her chin dipped into the high-zipped neck of her coat.

"Let's check with the upstairs tenants," Roman

said, setting back toward the front of the house. "Careful. The steps are icy."

He held out his hand to Ella, steadying her on the slick steps, then rang the bell. Seconds later, a young woman peeked through the glass side pane of the door, a guarded expression on her face. "No solicitors," she said. "Sorry."

"We're not selling anything," Roman said. "Just looking for Wes Bentley. He works with my friend over at Graceway."

Ella waved and moved closer. "We haven't heard from him in a few days and wanted to check on him," she added.

The woman opened the door and stepped onto the porch, pulling the door shut behind her. "He moved out," she said, thin lips set in a deep frown. "Before the lease ended, too."

"When was that?" Roman asked.

"Two days ago."

"Any idea where he went?" Roman asked.

"If I did, I'd send him a bill. He was a month behind on his rent and still has two months left on his lease."

"That's a tough spot to be put in," Roman said. "When we find him, we'll let you know."

He thanked the woman for her time and set a hand under Ella's elbow, helping her down the steps to the idling car.

"Looks like someone just moved up a few steps

on the suspect list," Luke commented as he pulled away from the curb. "Now back to the house?"

"Yes," Ella answered.

"I'll call Tyler when we get back and put a bug in his ear about Wes," Roman said.

"It's been a long couple of days," Luke commented, glancing at them in the rearview. "Roman, why don't I drop you off at your place on the way?"

Roman straightened, recognizing Luke's veiled attempt at getting him to go home and rest.

"I'm fine."

"Fine? When's the last time you slept for more than four hours?"

He didn't know, actually. Maybe a week ago. Before Ella had shown up at his office on Friday, he'd just wrapped up a high-profile security job that had demanded a ton of overtime. He had to admit he wasn't at his best. He rubbed tension out of the back of his neck. "You have a point."

"I'm dropping you off," Luke said. "And I'm working your shift."

"I think I'll take you up on that," he conceded.

Roman didn't need his whole shift taken, but he wasn't going to argue the point with Luke. He'd just take a shower and a few hours of sleep and head back to Julia Camden's house when he could think straight again.

Hours later, Ella quietly shut her bedroom door and reluctantly pulled out her flight information and her cell phone. It had been a long, emotional day. She had spent hours online pouring over Graceway's financial records and highlighting questionable transactions. She couldn't do much with it until she spoke with her mom or Jim, and she wondered if she was just wasting her time. If the files TechSavvy had recovered included Graceway's financial records and disclosures, she only needed to wait until tomorrow to get a look at the information. Still, she hadn't been able to help herself. She'd needed to do *something*. For now, the only thing she could do was cancel tomorrow's trip, which felt like the opposite of taking action.

It had taken days to plan the trip, but it only took a matter of minutes to cancel it. Ella tucked the boarding pass back in her filled suitcase. She'd been all ready to go. Tomorrow, she supposed, she'd unpack. For now, she needed sleep.

At least, she hoped that was what she needed. Her symptoms had been worsening since the fire this morning. Every couple of hours she'd had a lapse of confusion. She didn't dare talk to anyone about it. She'd be whisked back to the doctor, and he'd just increase her meds, which made her nauseous enough already.

She climbed into her old bed and pulled the covers up, overcome by a desperate sense of helplessness and anxiety. Her mind raced, trying to put all the pieces of the past weeks together in some sort of order that made sense and pointed to an answer. It was no use. Her mom would tell her she just needed a good cry and she'd feel better come the morning.

But Ella had shed enough tears to last the next decade. Crying didn't feel good or healing. It emptied her into a dark and hollow place and made it harder to come up for air. She rolled over, restless. Minutes ticked slowly by and she was sure sleep would never come. She'd been through this before. In the dark, she climbed out of bed, feeling around the surface of her desk where she'd left her sleeping pills. She'd used them regularly on nights like tonight—but still hadn't dared since the shooting weeks ago.

Tonight, though…

The house was secure. Roman had gone home for the night, but Ella was confident in his team and the extra security measures.

She found the bottle and took out a pill, swallowing it without water. Then she climbed back into bed and waited in the silent darkness until her eyes grew heavy and sleep finally overcame her.

When she next opened her eyes, her phone was vibrating, its glow illuminating the otherwise pitch-black room. She grabbed it, squinting at the text message as it came into focus.

Your Uber driver has arrived.

Uber driver? It was 3:45 a.m.

Her foggy mind reached for an explanation. The trip to Ethiopia! She darted up in bed. She'd overslept!

She flipped on her light and jumped out of bed, her foot slamming into the edge of her suitcase. Frantically, she looked around the room, trying to remember what she needed. She shoved her cell phone and charger in her purse, double-checked for her boarding pass and passport, crammed a hat over her head and grabbed her coat. Yanking on her sneakers, she opened her bedroom door and hurried down the dark hall, her suitcase rolling along hardwood. She reached for a light just as a figure rose from the living room couch.

Ella screamed, jumping back.

"Shh," Triss hissed, moving toward her.

Triss. Right. She'd forgotten. Her head throbbed, heartbeat frantic. She felt a little dizzy, truth be told. Something was seriously wrong.

"What's going on?" Ella asked, noting with alarm that Triss had drawn her gun.

Triss's attention was on the monitors. "Someone just pulled up," she whispered. "Luke's going around the back. Go into the bathroom and lock yourself in with your cell phone."

Ella laughed, her heart rate slowing down. "It's my Uber," she said just as the doorbell rang. She started to scoot around Triss, pushing aside the sense that she was missing something.

Triss blocked her path. "Your driver? Wait a minute. You and Roman agreed you would stay."

Ella frowned. Had they? Why couldn't she remember?

The driver knocked loudly and Ella maneuvered around Triss, unlocking the door and pulling it open. The alarm chime buzzed, the red light blinking. Triss quickly reset it. Ella's driver stood on the porch. "Can I help you with your bags?"

"She's not going," Triss said, her gun suddenly out of sight as she reached for the suitcase.

"I'm going," Ella insisted, but her voice faltered with rising uncertainty. She didn't remember any agreement with Roman. But that didn't mean she hadn't made one. Her memory lately had been spotty at best...

She hiked her purse up higher on her shoulder, searching desperately for context.

Triss yanked the suitcase across the entryway and took a seat on it. "Ethiopia's a difficult trip to manage without luggage," she said as she slid her phone out and put it to her ear.

The driver stood back uncertainly, his attention flicking between both women.

"Ella's on the run," Triss said into her phone, presumably to Roman. "She's decided to take herself off to Ethiopia all alone."

Ella stood nervously in the doorway, colder

by the minute. What was wrong? Something was wrong.

"I'll do what I can." Triss put the phone away and turned her attention to Ella. "I don't understand why you didn't just tell Roman you were going. I mean—"

"Hey!" a voice yelled from the side of the house. Luke appeared, backlit by the porch light, gun in hand.

"Whoa, whoa, whoa!" the Uber driver exclaimed, throwing his hands up in the air. He backed away from the house. "I'm out!" He turned and took off to his car, slamming the door and speeding away.

"Well," Triss said, standing and grabbing the suitcase handle. "I guess that settles it." She pushed the door shut and locked up.

"He would have planned to go with you, you know. Why let him believe you wouldn't go? It doesn't make any sense and..."

Triss continued her tirade as cold reality washed over Ella. She was right. Ella had canceled the flight. Roman was sending a team in her place.

Triss was staring at her with barely concealed contempt.

"You're right," Ella said.

Triss cocked her head to the side, her eyebrows shooting up. "I am," she agreed flatly. "So. What's going on?"

Ella wasn't quite ready to elaborate. It was past time to admit that the memory problem was not going away. In fact, it seemed to be getting worse as her stress level increased.

Triss shrugged at Ella's silence, clearly disgusted, and plopped herself into the reclining chair. "Roman will be here in a few minutes. He'll want an explanation."

Ella slumped into the couch. The last thing she needed at four o'clock in the morning was Roman's lecture. She wished she could somehow bypass his visit and go straight back to bed as if the past half hour had never happened. But moments later when Roman walked through the door, one look at his dark expression told Ella exactly what he thought of her actions this morning—and how intent he was on discussing them.

THIRTEEN

Roman closed the door behind him, not bothering to take off his boots or coat, and sat across from Ella.

"What were you thinking, Ell?" he asked.

"I'm so sorry," she said quietly. She sat stiffly on the couch, absently petting Isaac, who seemed to be snoozing through all the drama. Triss, Roman noticed, had made herself scarce.

Ella's silence stretched until Roman's patience ran out.

"You could have gotten yourself killed," he said, hearing the edge in his voice. But he couldn't curb it. "I don't get it—you asked for my help, but you don't seem to trust me enough to follow my lead."

Finally, Ella met his eyes. She looked as worn as Roman felt.

"I do trust you," she said.

"Then if you didn't like the plan, why didn't you tell me?" he persisted.

Her gaze slid away for a split second before returning to him. Something flashed in her eyes, a second of consideration. Her shoulders sagged just a little and she tugged on the white knit cap she wore, eyes downcast. "It was the memory thing again."

His eyes narrowed. "What do you mean?"

"Last night I took a sleeping pill for the first time in weeks. I had forgotten to cancel my Uber for the flight, so when my phone started buzzing to let me know the driver was here at three thirty…it took a while to figure out what was going on."

"That's one powerful sleeping pill," he said.

"It wasn't just that," she said. "It's been happening a lot."

"A lot. As in…?"

"At least a couple times a day," she admitted.

"Why didn't you tell me?" he asked. "You agreed you would."

She stared at him, dark eyes flashing with… what? Anger? Embarrassment? Anxiety?

"I didn't want to waste any more time with doctors for a condition that only time can heal. And the medicine doesn't help. It just makes everything fuzzier."

"It's not like I would have forced you to go to the hospital," he said, trying to understand her logic but unable. "The main reason I wanted you to keep me in the loop was so we could better protect you. The more information we have, the safer you are."

"I realize that now," she said. "I'm sorry."

"What medications are you on exactly?" Roman asked.

"They have me on Ritalin to help with my memory and Prozac for my alleged depression." She rolled her eyes. "Other than that, just Ambien for sleep, but with the exception of tonight, I haven't taken it since the night I was shot."

"It wouldn't hurt to talk to your doctor," Roman said. "Other medicine may work better."

"I'm more inclined to just stop the meds cold turkey," she said, a streak of stubbornness in her eyes.

"I don't know about that, Ella."

She fell silent again and he sighed, letting the matter drop for now. "Look. If you're bent on going to Ethiopia, we'll make a plan. In the meantime, don't go anywhere."

"I'm not planning to, trust me," she said.

He didn't respond, just stood and left the living room, his adrenaline still coming down from the early morning scare. He absolutely could not trust Ella. Not for now, at least. Whether she'd had a memory lapse or made a poor decision, trusting her could put Ella and the whole team in danger.

He made his way to the kitchen and Triss looked up from where she was sitting at the table. "Everything okay?" she asked.

"Just need some air." Roman let himself out into the backyard and into a morning that was still and cold, the yard pristinely white under the new floodlights. The morning could have gone in a much different direction, and he was still reeling from what might have happened.

He stepped into the yard and walked a slow loop around the perimeter, considering the events of the past few days and praying for new insight because it was getting more difficult by the hour to keep Ella safe.

As much as he didn't want to admit it, he knew Ella was right that a trip to Ethiopia was in order. She'd had a ticket to fly out there before she was shot, and she couldn't remember what the purpose of the trip had been. But with her mom in a coma at the time, and all of Graceway in Ella's hands, she must have had a compelling reason to want to go.

And all he could figure out was that someone else must have had a compelling reason to keep her from going.

He was lost in thought when the back door opened sometime later.

"I guess there'd be no convincing you to go back home at this point," Luke said, appearing in the doorway.

"I've got it from here," Roman agreed. "Thanks for taking over tonight, though."

"Any time," Luke said, joining Roman in the

yard. "You've been out here walking laps for a while. How can I help?"

"Is your passport current?" Roman asked.

If the question surprised him, Luke didn't show it. "Yes."

"Do you have any big plans for the week?"

"I'll clear my social calendar," Luke responded with sarcasm.

Roman laughed. They both lived and breathed their work, their social calendars nonexistent.

"I guess this means we're going to Ethiopia," Luke said.

"I don't see a way around it," Roman agreed.

"I'll get packing. Need me to do anything else before the trip?"

Roman thought for a moment. "Actually, yes. Check the medicine cabinet and see where Ella gets her prescriptions filled. Then call in the refills and grab them for her? Something tells me she won't have enough time to do it herself." Or inclination, for that matter.

"Not a problem. I'll see you tomorrow."

An hour later, Roman was at the kitchen table booking tickets online when Triss appeared in the doorway. "Got a sec?" she asked.

"Sure. What's up?"

She crossed the small kitchen and held her phone out to him. "Check this out."

He took the phone and read the news headline she'd pulled up.

"'Like Father, Like Son? Local Pastor Falls From Grace.'" He glanced up at Triss.

"Keep reading," she said.

"'Hank Wright, popular pastor of Anchor of Hope Fellowship in Annapolis, hasn't released any response yet to recent allegations of extra-marital affairs.'"

"Pastor Wright?" Ella asked, emerging from the hallway, her cheeks flushed from sleep.

Roman looked back at the phone, finding his place again. "'A woman has come forward claiming an ongoing relationship with the Annapolis pastor, and other tips are pointing to a possible affair he had with the late Marilynn Rice, who was killed last week during a home burglary.'"

"Unbelievable," Ella said.

Triss shrugged. "Is it?"

Roman looked up, saw something in her dark brown eyes—a hidden hurt deeper than the cool cynicism she portrayed.

"You don't think so?" Ella asked her.

"Not really." Triss held out her hand for the phone and Roman gave it back.

Ella looked like she was about to press further, but Triss was already slipping out of the kitchen and away from a conversation she clearly didn't want to have.

"That was cryptic," Ella murmured. She pulled

her sweater tighter around her middle and leaned against the door frame, her expression puzzled. "I never saw the pastor and Marilynn together," she said.

"That's generally what happens when people are having an affair," Roman pointed out.

"I know…"

"But?"

"I just can't imagine Marilynn…it seems so out of character."

Because of his line of work, nothing surprised Roman anymore, but he figured saying so wouldn't do much good. "I wonder how JT's going to take this news," he said.

"He'll be devastated," Ella said. "Maybe I should call and check on him today."

"I'd give it some time," Roman suggested. "He's already grieving. If he's read this, his pride may be hurt, as well."

"You're probably right," Ella said, still looking miffed by the whole situation.

Meanwhile, Roman's mind was working overtime. If the pastor was having extramarital affairs, if he had possibly been involved in murder, there was no limit to what he could be capable of. He filed the thought away for later.

"In any case, we have a lot of ground to cover today," Roman told her. "I just booked our flights for tomorrow."

"What?"

"It seems like an important piece of this puzzle might be in Ethiopia," he said. "And, if not, at least you can get your eyes on the situation with the residential center to get a clearer idea of the resources they'll be needing. We leave at 4:00 a.m. Luke's coming with us for backup."

He thought she'd be elated, but she looked like she was about to cry.

"Thank you," she said quietly, and slipped out of the kitchen and down the hall.

He stopped himself from following her. He'd allowed himself to get too close already, which was dangerous in more ways than one. It was time to step back and be a professional.

Ella sat on the edge of her bed, a hollow loneliness taking hold. Even after everything, Roman was as steady as ever. It had never been so painfully clear to her exactly what she had lost.

She stared out the window at the quiet street as morning rose. Flurries still fell outside and Ella's memory slipped off to the day she regretted most in her life.

It had been snowing that afternoon, too. A beautiful, crisp, winter snow.

She and Roman had walked Brooklyn to the last classes of her day—two back-to-back classes that ran from three to six. Her ex had been threatening her, and the family had made a pact that she'd go nowhere alone until the situation had been ironed out.

Ella had planned to get some work done at the library and then meet Roman for coffee until it was time to get Brooklyn after her classes. Only, it had looked like a winter wonderland and studying was the last thing Ella had wanted to do.

"Let's go see a movie," she suggested.

He didn't really want to, she could tell. He was tired after a long day of work. He smiled anyway—a tired smile—and linked his arm in hers.

"Let's go," he agreed, and brushed a warm kiss at her temple as they changed direction toward the parking lot.

It was forty-five minutes into the movie when Brooklyn texted Ella to let her know that classes had been canceled. Ella had felt the phone vibrate in her pocket, but had waited until a convenient spot in the movie to leave the theater and check her texts. Grabbing their popcorn carton to refill, she'd read her texts as she'd walked to the lobby.

Truth be told, she didn't really believe Brooklyn was in serious danger. Her ex was a coward if ever there was one. The verbal abuse had been sickening, but he had never been physically abusive. Plus, he'd gone quiet in recent weeks. So she'd texted back that they were at a movie and asked if Brooklyn could find someone else to walk her back.

That was the part Roman didn't know about.

She'd gone back to the movie and didn't check her phone for another fifteen minutes. By then, Brooklyn had found another friend to walk her, so Ella had simply whispered to Roman about the change of plans. She didn't mention that she had instigated the change. He'd been uneasy. She'd reassured him.

If only...

Roman's anxiety had only worsened until Ella finally, reluctantly, had agreed to leave the movie and head back to campus. But they had wasted too much time. When they'd arrived at the dorm, Brooklyn was dead.

Logic told her that she couldn't have known what the day would bring. But grief and guilt wouldn't let her forgive herself. The familiar ache of regret rose up and Ella forced herself to stand, shutting the blinds to the memories.

She needed to shower and change. They had a busy day ahead and a big trip the next morning. She was actually relieved about the turn of events. She was almost desperate to get on a plane, to do *something* tangible toward figuring out what was happening at Graceway. And Graceway's Ethiopian program seemed to be a mysterious piece of the puzzle.

By noon they had already accomplished a day's worth of work. Ella had the flash drive from Tech-Savvy in hand, along with a newly forwarded link to the backup files that she had somehow missed when they'd originally been emailed to her. Officer Goodson and his team had reported back on the findings at the scene of the fire—components of an explosive device were identified by the fire marshal, but it would be a while before they had more answers. Current speculation was that the device had been planted under a couple of floorboards.

That would explain why Roman hadn't spotted anything unusual during his walk-through before the fire. The knowledge brought a mixture of reassurance and anxiety.

But there was no time to dwell on anxiety right now. Their next stop was the church, where Ella planned to meet with Jim Cannon to discuss Graceway's finances. Her mother had already frozen the accounts stateside, and was working on freezing the ones in Ethiopia. She had also added Ella as a joint-owner of the accounts so she could get involved with the financial issues. Ella hoped Jim would be able to advise her on some of the discrepancies she'd found.

She stared out the window, listening as Roman and Connor chatted up front about Connor's new grandbaby. When they'd left the house earlier, Ella had scooted into the back seat, expecting Roman to get in beside her, but he had closed the door and taken a seat up front with Connor, a retired police officer who had joined Shield last year.

It hadn't escaped Ella's attention that Roman had kept his distance from her since the morning's incident. He'd stayed at her side, but he'd been careful not to touch her. She'd gotten used to the warmth of his hand at her back, the protective grip of his fingers entwined with hers. The absence of his touch left her cold and uncertain of where they stood. At the same time, she was relieved he was taking a step back. She knew she needed to tell Roman the whole truth of what had happened the night of Brooklyn's death, and rekindling their relationship would only make the second loss more devastating.

The car pulled past the church, where a half dozen news crews littered the front lot.

"I've got Bryan in there now getting access through the back," Roman said. The church ran a preschool in one wing, where they would enter to connect to the church offices.

Roman used his radio to direct his team to their locations as Connor pulled the car up to the rear entrance. The three exited the vehicle quickly and entered the building together, Connor taking the lead. Inside, they passed the preschool reception area and continued down several long corridors of empty classrooms.

"You really know your way around this place," Ella commented.

"That's my job," he said simply.

His cordial tone hurt, but Ella knew she was just being overly sensitive. It wasn't as if—

"Shh…" Connor stopped, his hand up. The distinct sound of hushed voices filtered into the hallway.

Roman motioned for Ella to walk behind him and carried on down the hall, slower now, his footsteps treading quietly along the carpet.

They were nowhere near the offices yet, but in an area of the church not normally used during the work day. As they slowly made their way down the hall, the voices grew more distinct—a male and a female, their words quiet but harsh. An argument of some kind, coming from a closed classroom. Roman motioned for Connor to slow down.

"—do this to me?" the female snapped.

"Patty, honey. You've got to believe me."

Ella stopped at the doorway behind Roman, immediately realizing who had taken refuge in the quiet classroom. Hank and his wife. From what Ella could gather, the news had come out while Hank was already at the office. Maybe his wife had come to confront him. Neither probably wanted to leave the premises under all that media scrutiny.

Roman motioned across the hall to Connor and the three continued toward the offices.

As they rounded the next corner, they finally

reached the main lobby and entered the church offices. The secretary, Lacey, smiled guardedly at them. "Can I help you?"

"We were hoping to speak with Jim," Roman said.

"He's in a meeting right now," she said. "Can I let him know you stopped by?"

"We can wait," Roman said.

"Well, that's fine. I'm not sure how long—"

"I appreciate the time," a Southern voice chirped from down the hall, and Autumn appeared, Jim at her side. He was smiling broadly, almost admiringly at her, and Ella's eyes narrowed on the two. Was there something there that she was missing?

"Absolutely," Jim said, his smile falling a little when he saw Roman and Ella in the lobby.

"Hey, you two," Autumn said casually.

Ella didn't miss the surprise in her eyes. "Hey to you," Ella said. "Didn't expect to see you here."

"Autumn was gracious enough to come help me with my ancient computer," Jim explained. "She's a whiz with this stuff, you know."

Autumn shrugged with a grin.

"You picked the right person to call," Ella said, trying to read the situation.

"What about you?" Autumn asked.

"Wes has disappeared," Ella explained. "We wanted to see if Jim had any insight."

Jim looked perplexed. "Wes? I barely knew the guy."

"Really?" Ella asked. "I assumed you knew him, since he took over your position."

Jim shook his head. "Pastor Wright offered me the position here. When I expressed concern over leaving your mom in a bind, he said he had someone in mind who could take over. Your mom hired him on reference alone."

"That doesn't sound like my mom," Ella said.

"It was a tough time for her, Ella," Jim said. His voice was kind but she was sure she detected censure in his tone. As if she should have known, should have been here.

She *should* have.

"Wow," Autumn said. "Just disappeared? That's suspicious." She looked thoughtful for a moment. "Want me to take a look at his computer? See what I can recover?"

"It's a loss because of the fire," Ella said.

"Convenient," Autumn said. "Oh, speaking of which…" She dug into her jeans pocket and produced a folded sheet of paper, handing it to Ella. "I finished the list of people who had access to your mom's house and Graceway—though we're missing names because we don't have the visitor log anymore."

Ella accepted the paper, unfolded it and scanned familiar names, no one standing out to her. "Thanks," she said, passing it back to Autumn. "Do you think you could drop this by the station for Officer Goodson? I haven't had a chance to tell you, but we're actually heading out tomorrow for Ethiopia."

"Sure, I can do that." Autumn tucked the list back into her pocket and grinned toward Roman. "So, she finally wore you down," she commented.

"Something like that," he said with good humor.

"You need someone to help with Isaac?" Autumn asked Ella.

"Our team has it covered," Roman answered for her. "Shield will keep an eye on the house while we're gone."

"Okay, well, be safe." Autumn hugged Ella tight and then waved goodbye to Roman and Jim before leaving the office.

Jim stood at Lacey's desk, his attention on Ella. "So, I assumed you'll need me to fill in for Wes while you're gone?" he asked.

"Everything should be in order for the week, but if you could be on call if a problem comes up, I'd appreciate it."

"Of course."

"I really appreciate it. But there's something else, too." Ella reached into her bag and pulled out the folded manila envelope she'd stuffed with printouts from bank records. "I have questions," she said.

He motioned them to follow him into his office, a comfortable space with mahogany furniture accented with a rug and curtains in warm gold and cream tones. Ella and Roman took the two seats across from Jim's desk and she spread out the pages on the surface so Jim could read the itemized list as she explained her concerns.

She'd barely gotten started when she realized Jim had stopped looking at the pages in front of him and was instead looking at her quizzically. She paused, waiting for what he obviously wanted to say.

"We've had this conversation before," he said, his tone careful and not accusing.

"What do you mean?"

"You don't remember?" he asked. "I mean…" He glanced down at the papers. "There are more transactions now, but your concerns were the same when you met with me weeks ago."

"When did we meet?" Ella asked, heart pounding with the suspicion that she may be finally tapping into something crucial.

"The beginning of last month," he answered, his expression perplexed.

Before the shooting, then.

"I'm sorry, Jim. I've had trouble with my memory since I was shot. Was anyone else in the meeting?"

"No. You'd contacted me that morning and asked if you could bring something by at lunch. You said you felt more comfortable talking with me about it than Wes, because you didn't know him well."

"Did anything come of the meeting?" she asked.

"I advised you to ask Wes about several of the items, and you called me the next day and told me you were relieved because there had been logical explanations for all of the questionable transactions."

"What were the explanations?" Ella asked.

"I don't recall everything," Jim said. "But the transfers to Ethiopia were to cover building costs for the new programs, and the withdrawals state-side were provisions for the residential tenants."

Ella slumped back in her seat, miffed by the entire story. Was she really seeing problems where none existed?

"Are you all right, Ella?" Jim asked, watching her with fatherly concern.

She wasn't, but she nodded anyway, grabbing her purse and standing. "Mystery solved, I guess," she said. But gut instinct told her that was far from the truth.

FOURTEEN

Jim stood and opened the door for Roman and Ella to exit. "If you find anything else you want me to look at, just call."

"I will," Ella agreed, brushing past him into the office lobby. "I might need help removing Wes from Graceway's accounts," she added.

"I can get that taken care of for you," he said. "Strangest thing how he's just up and disappeared."

"Who's up and disappeared?" Pastor Wright asked, walking in on their conversation suddenly.

He looked neat and polished as usual, but tension lined his face, his eyes troubled.

"Wes Bentley." Roman filled him in. "Have you heard from him?"

"No. But then, I didn't know him that well."

"Wait, I thought you recommended him to my mom," Ella said. "Isn't that what you told me, Jim?"

Jim nodded. "That's what I remembered."

"I did recommend him to your mom. Doug vouched for him, and that was good enough for me. Is there something else going on aside from his absence?"

"More like his disappearing act," Ella said.

Just then Patty Wright stormed into the lobby, her face flushed and eyes blazing. She nodded to the group, but didn't actually greet them. Instead she skirted around them and down the hall, entering the pastor's office where she was likely waiting to give him several more pieces of her mind.

The pastor sighed and followed his wife, shutting the door behind him.

Ella followed Roman and Connor back through the church, the way they'd entered, her mind racing. In the past few days she hadn't been discovering anything new at all—she had simply been rediscovering the same problems she'd found weeks ago. And she had met with both Jim and Wes to discuss them. Had her mom also found those problems? Is that why she'd been run off the road? And what about Marilynn? Was the pastor somehow involved in the attacks? It seemed unlikely, but so did his affair in the first place.

She rolled the questions around in her head during the ten-minute drive back to her mom's house, but she didn't get any closer to any satisfying answers.

Roman opened the car door for her. "I'm going home to pack my gear," he said. "Connor's taking my place tonight so I can catch some sleep before the trip tomorrow. Need anything, let me know."

"Sounds good," she said, talking to his back as he closed her door and headed to the driver's side. She walked with Connor up to the house, telling herself not to be disappointed. Roman had a job to do, and it didn't involve sticking around Ella 24/7.

Several hours later, Ella was more than ready for the trip. She had created an agenda for each day they would be in Ethiopia, and she had also spent a lot of nervous energy reviewing Graceway's finances, trying to figure out what she'd missed. Jim had also texted her to let her know he'd removed Wes Bentley from the bank accounts. The only thing left to do before the trip was pay a visit to Ella's mom.

Ella had been looking forward to visiting her mother up until the moment her fingers touched the handle of the hospital room door. It occurred to her then that her mother probably would not be thrilled about the impending trip, but she'd have to tell her. Otherwise, she'd have no other way to explain why she wouldn't be visiting for the next several days.

Seeing no way around it, she entered the room.

"I'll be just outside," Connor said, pulling the door shut behind her.

Her mother appeared to be sleeping peacefully, with only an IV dripping fluids. All her other tubes had been removed and color had returned to her cheeks. "Hey, Mom," Ella said quietly, gently rubbing her forearm.

Her mom's eyes blinked opened and she smiled tiredly. "Ella, you're sweet to come visit again."

"Mom, I've been here every day for weeks," she said. "I'd be here all day every day if I could. How are you feeling?"

"Ready to go home," her mother responded, pressing a button on her bed to elevate her upper body. "Pass me that water?" she asked.

Ella reached over and poured ice water from a pitcher into a foam cup, handing it to her mom.

"Hopefully they'll discharge you soon," Ella said and then plowed right into the reason for her visit. "I wanted to let you know that I'm leaving tomorrow for Ethiopia."

Her mom didn't appear as shocked or worried as Ella had imagined she'd be.

"I'd tell you not to go, but I can see you're set on the plan."

"I am. I'm determined to figure out what's going on. You've worked too long and too hard for Graceway to fall apart."

Her mother took another few sips of water and passed the empty cup to Ella.

"I'm planning to step down, Ella."

For a moment, her words hung between them, Ella trying to make sense of what her mother was saying.

"Retire? But you love Graceway! You—"

"I do love Graceway," her mother interrupted. "And I'm not retiring just yet. I'd like to transition it over to a new executive director, though. I'll make sure the offices get rebuilt here, and that the families at our program in Ethiopia are taken care of. But it's obvious I can't keep up running it the way it needs to be. Not at my age and in my health."

"Don't make any big decisions just yet," Ella said lightly, not sure what to do with her mother's announcement. "Spend a little time recovering and getting some rest. You'll probably feel differently when—"

"I've made up my mind," her mom said firmly, cutting Ella off again. "It's time. I knew it before the accident, and it's even clearer now. I may even just transfer ownership to the church."

It probably wasn't a good time to bring up the scandal in the news about Pastor Wright, so Ella just nodded. "You have plenty of time to figure out the details," she said. She expected her mother to be devastated at the prospect, but she looked entirely at ease.

"It was a beautiful time in my life," her mom said. "But God has placed me in a new season. I'm ready to leave the leadership to someone else. Marilynn and I have talked about doing some overseas mission work together, maybe a little traveling. This life here is so short."

"You're pretty amazing, Mom," Ella said, her throat tight. She knew she needed to tell her mom about Marilynn, but couldn't bring herself to do it just yet. Not when her mother was still so weak, her health so fragile.

"Oh, I don't know about that," her mom said with a short laugh.

"I just wish I had a fraction of your faith."

Her mother searched her face, her expression considering. "I fight doubt as often as the next person," she said.

"But you always find a reason to hope."

"Don't you?"

"Not always," Ella admitted, feeling unusually emotional.

Her mom shifted and settled her hand over Ella's. "What's going on, sweetie?"

"I don't know, Mom...ever since Brooklyn died, you know I've struggled."

"It's hard to make sense of tragedy," her mom agreed.

"Sometimes, I think it's impossible. The other day, when Roman and I were trapped in the fire... I really thought we weren't going to make it." She took a shaky breath and her mom squeezed her hand. "I prayed we would escape, and I don't think I've ever prayed so hard."

"And you made it out," her mom pointed out. "He always hears us."

"We did. But Brooklyn didn't. Her entire family spent months praying for her safety and she was still murdered. If prayers were answered on the measure of our faith, she would be alive. And I wouldn't be. How does God choose? And why even pray if He's already decided the final outcome?"

Her mom was quiet for a moment and then smiled gently. "Those are big questions, Ella. Age-old ones that no one ever has a satisfying answer to."

"I was hoping you would," she said with a small laugh.

"You know what? I've seen God answer prayers in big ways in my life. I've been through times when He seemed silent and I doubted His compassion and goodness. But on the other side of all that prayer time, I started to see something over the years."

"What?"

"I think sometimes God hears our prayers and answers them in mighty ways—humanly impossible ways—to show His power and His mercy, to increase our faith and draw other people to Him." She paused, in thought, and then continued. "But no one escapes suffering because we live in a fallen world. Sometimes, for reasons we won't understand this side of Heaven, He hears our prayers and offers us His sufficiency instead of what our human hearts desire most. It's in our deepest losses and heartaches that we learn to fully rely on Him."

Her mother's answer was beautifully simple and faith-filled, but it felt too much like surrender without a guaranteed happy ending. Then again, happy endings were never a guarantee, and every waking morning was a gift. Maybe there was a certain freedom in surrendering to that realization, to trusting a God whose vision was eternal instead of temporal. But surrender had never been part of Ella's vocabulary.

She could see her mother was getting sleepy, so she leaned over and pressed a kiss to her cheek. "I wish I had the kind of peace you have," she said. "Love you, Mom. I'll be back this weekend." She let herself out of the room, but her mother's words weren't lost on her and Ella tucked them away to revisit later when she was alone.

Every house on the street was dark, a handful of porch lights standing guard in the night, the working streetlights few and far between. But behind the blinds of every window at Julia Camden's home, a light was on. Ella would be inside, waiting to leave for the airport.

Roman parked the car and stared at the house for a few moments. He'd had a long talk with God this morning as he'd readied to leave the house. A flight to Africa with Ella left too many loopholes for danger. For one, he had a small team and limited knowledge of their destination.

The second problem was that he couldn't fly armed into Ethiopia. Roman had confidence in his fighting skills, but he'd feel a lot better with a weapon.

Ella was dead-set on going, though, and he couldn't say he blamed her. In her position, for the sake of her mom's business, and in the face of the attacks she'd endured, her desire to investigate on her own made sense.

It also put him on edge. He'd rather go on this trip alone, but Ella was a wild card and would probably be safer with him in Ethiopia than in the States with a team of his people who barely knew her.

He turned off the engine, the heat cutting out, stillness settling around him as he wondered yet again if he was making the right decision.

The front blinds shifted and Triss peeked out, spurring Roman into motion. The time for second-guessing had long passed.

He climbed out of the car, pocketed his keys and walked up to the house as Triss opened the door for him.

Clattering came from the kitchen, along with the scent of cinnamon and coffee. Ella peeked out of the kitchen with a smile that brought back all the old feelings Roman had been fighting.

"Cinnamon rolls just came out."

"I don't need to be told twice," Triss said, and Roman followed her to the kitchen.

"We have a few minutes," Ella said. "Sit, have some breakfast."

She scooted past him with a tray of glistening cinnamon rolls that looked decidedly unlike the kind Roman sometimes baked out of a can from the grocery store when his nieces and nephews came to visit.

"Those look great," he said. "But you didn't have to make breakfast."

Ella set the tray down over some potholders on the table and moved back to the kitchen, opening the fridge. She didn't look his way. "You're traveling to Africa with me with one day's notice. The least I could do was feed you."

"She's been cooking since two," Triss said faintly.

Roman's gaze cut to Ella as she came back to the table, toting a bowl of hard-boiled eggs, a carton of orange juice and a bowl of grapes.

He reached over the counter and pulled out a stack of plates. "Why'd you get up at two?"

"It takes a while for the dough to rise and then to make the rolls," she said.

"No, I mean what possessed you to get up at two to make cinnamon rolls? From scratch?" He set the plates at the table and took a seat.

"I had a craving," she said with a shrug. She'd donned a navy ball cap, a gray T-shirt and a pair of jeans. And with cheeks rosy from the warmth of the kitchen, eyes shimmering slate-blue, she'd never looked more beautiful to him.

"Also, I couldn't sleep," she added, pulling out a seat for herself. "Because of this," she said, setting a manila folder in front of his plate.

He reached over and flipped the folder open, recognizing at first glance some of the bank records they'd retrieved yesterday afternoon.

He lifted the stack and skimmed through, noting multicolored highlighting and notes neatly written in margins. "You stayed up all night doing this, didn't you?" he asked.

She nodded. "You know how I get sometimes. I dug through everything on that flash drive and organized all the information I had pulled from the financial records."

"What'd you find?" he asked, setting the folder down and taking a bite of the cinnamon roll. It tasted like something fresh out of a bakery oven.

She riffled through the folder and pulled out a sheet she'd marked with a blue sticky tab.

"I finally got a handle on the big picture," she said. "The bottom line is that money's disappearing." She pointed to a table she'd created and showed him several funds set up through Graceway's bank account. She'd listed their balances from every quarter over the past three years.

"See the trend?"

It was easy to spot with how she'd presented the information. "All the accounts were steady or rising until February. Stateside, at least," he said.

"Right. My mom got sick a few months before that. Wes started working at Graceway that December."

"How did no one notice?" Roman asked.

"February ninth was the last IRS audit," Ella said. "It's not until a couple weeks afterward that the questionable transactions start to show up. Plus, on the surface, it looks legit."

She set two printed emails in front of Roman. "My mom agreed to temporarily funnel increased funds to Graceway Ethiopia—a 1.2 million-dollar increase spread over the next year. But all the transfers to the Ethiopia account add up to nearly two million already, and it's only been nine months."

"Which accounts for the reduced funding here," Roman said.

Roman glanced through some of the pages, then set the folder down again and shook his head. "A veterinarian who could double as a police detective and bakes like you attended culinary school. You're a woman of many talents, Ella," he said, impressed by her finds and hopeful that her discovery would finally give the police a strong lead.

"There's something else, too. Six months ago,

there were several new hires in the Ethiopia program and their salaries are quite high. I texted my mom about it, and she doesn't recall new employees."

"Who was in charge of the hiring process?" Roman asked.

"Someone named Melody Lyles. She was the first new hire in Ethiopia—payroll lists her as the HR manager, but Mom doesn't recognize the name."

"We'll want to talk to her. This gives us a lot more to go on, but it still feels like we're missing something critical, doesn't it?" Roman asked.

She nodded. "Hopefully we'll find it on our trip this week." She leaned over him to grab the carton of orange juice.

He caught the scent of vanilla and flour before she settled back in her seat to pour a glass.

"Want another?" she asked, gesturing to the tray of cinnamon rolls, but his attention had shifted to the curve of her lips. Every instinct longed to lean in and kiss her again, to forget all the complications of this week—and the grief of years past—and to start over again.

"I'll take one if he won't," Triss said bluntly, and Roman realized he'd been silent a few seconds too long.

The pink in Ella's cheeks deepened and she scooted her chair back from the table, reality settling in around them.

He'd be professional if it killed him, but he sure hoped they'd get to the bottom of things by the end of the week, because the longer he spent with Ella, the more time he wanted to spend with her, and the harder it was going to be to say good-bye again.

Ella took a sip of her juice and then stood, crossing the kitchen and opening a cabinet. She pulled out her two prescription bottles. "I forgot to call in the scripts," she said, opening one of the bottles.

"I had Luke grab them for you yesterday," Roman said. "Hold on."

He went into the living room and retrieved the bottles from his carry-on, returning to the kitchen in moments. "Here you go," he said, passing the medication to Ella.

"That's a relief, thanks. I'll just combine the bottles."

She poured the last three capsules from one bottle into her hand and started to dump them into the new bottle, but paused.

"That's strange."

Roman leaned closer to get a look and she held her palm out to him.

At first, he didn't know what she was referring to, but when he looked closer, he saw it. One of the pills had a slight crease at its center.

He took the green Prozac capsule from her

and inspected it. "Anything wrong with the others?" he asked.

"No," Ella said. "But wait." She pulled a pill from the new bottle and set it in her palm as a comparison. The length of the capsule was noticeably different.

She looked up at Roman, horror dawning in her eyes. "Someone tampered with these."

"Looks like it," Roman said grimly, pulling out his phone and snapping some photos, which he then sent to Tyler Goodson. He looked at Triss, the silent observer this morning. "Can you get these to the police station this morning?"

"Of course," she said. "Who picked up your medication last time, Ella?"

"Autumn," Ella answered.

Roman's suspicion toward Ella's friend grew exponentially, especially considering her offer to pick up the scripts again the other day.

"I wish we could stay and figure this out, but we don't have time," Roman said to Ella. "If you're about ready, we'd better get going."

Ella closed the prescription bottles and slid them over to Triss. "May as well have it all checked out," she said. "I'm staying away from medicine for a few days." Then she tucked plastic wrap over the pan of cinnamon rolls. "Take a couple, Triss, and maybe drop some off at Hunter's for his kids?"

"If any are left by the time I see him again, sure," Triss said with a hint of a smile.

The three worked quickly to clean up the kitchen and moments later they stepped out into the bitter cold, their breath swirling white around them.

Luke was already waiting in the SUV and Triss took the driver's seat as Roman and Ella scooted into the middle row. Roman scrolled on his phone, looking at the flight itinerary.

"We'll arrive in Addis close to noon tomorrow," Roman said to Ella. "I've scheduled a driver to meet us and take us to the guesthouse. Depending on security, though, we may move to a hotel after the first night."

"I'll do whatever you think is best."

Roman laughed.

"What?"

"What I thought was best was you staying home, but here we are."

"I thought we—"

"I know, I know," he said, cutting her off. "I understand the whys. I just wish there was a better way to get this done."

FIFTEEN

It was noon and dismal when they arrived the next day in Addis Ababa, Ethiopia, nearly two by the time they'd checked in at the guesthouse.

Ella changed into khakis and a white tank top, exchanging sneakers for sandals. She had high hopes for the day, and it felt good to be doing something tangible for Graceway. Actually, she felt great physically, too—even after nearly twenty hours of travel. She hadn't had any nausea this morning and she felt more clear-headed than she had in a long while. She was sure it wasn't a coincidence that she hadn't taken any of her pills in more than two days.

It was muggy in her room and she went to the window, shoving it open. A humid breeze filtered in as she looked out over the rooftops of the quiet city beyond. Dirt roads converged with paved roads converged with alleys and buildings and houses. A pungent scent wafted in from outside—not unpleasant, but unfamiliar. A tap sounded at her door and she opened it to Roman, who handed her a coffee.

"I figured you could use some caffeine," he said. "Ready to get this show on the road?"

He was casual in a dark pair of jeans and black polo, but Ella's breath caught anyway. She needed to settle things with Graceway quickly and go back to Colorado because she didn't see herself ever getting beyond the attraction she had to Roman.

Meanwhile he was all cordial kindness and professional courtesy.

"No coffee?" he asked, and she realized she'd been standing in the door a moment too long.

"Thank you," she said, collecting herself and accepting the warm cup. She snagged her purse and phone and followed him out to the waiting van.

Luke was already in the front passenger seat of the old, white cargo van, which had no seat belts or air conditioner. Their driver, Bereket, was a tall, slender man with a bald head, dark skin and a brilliant white smile. He spoke limited English, but was incredibly friendly and hospitable. His driving was impressive as he navigated streets with no signs or speed limits, sharing the road with cyclists, walkers and even donkeys.

It was only a thirty-minute drive to Graceway Village Ethiopia, and as the driver pulled up to the gates, Ella's heart sank.

The building had been completely destroyed. Dozens of workers traipsed through the charred remains, gathering trash and cleaning up debris. It was obvious the whole building would have to be leveled and rebuilt.

A young woman with thick, beautiful braids crossed over to them as they stepped out of the van. "I'm Almaz," she said, her English lovely with a lilting accent. She reached out a hand to Ella first. "You must be Ms. Camden. So pleased to meet you."

Ella introduced Roman and Luke, and then looked beyond Almaz at the remains of Graceway. "I'm so sorry this happened," Ella said. "We're here to help. No one was hurt?"

Almaz shook her head. "Thankfully, everyone escaped. God is good. Here, I will show you."

The wreckage was unredeemable, yet dozens of workers combed through it, separating what was lost from what could possibly be salvaged. Ella noticed immediately the many mothers working alongside children to clean up the remains of the building. Toddlers and preschoolers climbed over debris with bare feet, while babies snuggled content in slings on strong backs. It wasn't safe for the kids to be walking in, and it certainly wasn't safe for them to be breathing in the dust. Ella made a mental note to take care of that problem first.

"Do we know yet how the fire started?" Ella

asked as they came full circle and wound up back where Bereket was waiting for them.

Almaz paused, eyes dark with what could only be described as fear. "It was deliberate," she said, her accent pronouncing each syllable carefully. "In the middle of the night, someone bordered the facility with gasoline and then set the fire."

Roman let out a low whistle.

"How did everyone get out?" Ella asked.

Almaz raised her arms, motioning around her. "The community. That's the way we do things here. They see fire and everyone comes to help." She shook her head. "God did not allow evil to prevail."

Her words reminded Ella of what her mother had said about God answering prayer to show His power. "We're working on a plan to extend the lodging for your families during the rebuild," she told Almaz. "In the meantime, I'd like to purchase masks and shoes for everyone who's working to clean up the debris. Can you tell me where I can find those items?"

Almaz smiled brightly. "Wonderful, wonderful. I will ask Bereket to take you." She seemed to hesitate and then added, "We feel reassured by your presence. Since funding has been down and we have had to scale back, concerns had begun to grow among our staff and residents."

"Scale back in what way?" Ella asked, alarmed.

Graceway's Ethiopian bank account was healthy and should be providing well.

"Oh, do not worry—we have not been uncomfortable," Almaz assured her. "Not as much fresh produce, fewer clothing, not taking on any new families. But Melody assured us that we would see improvement soon and we can—"

"Melody Lyles?" Ella asked, remembering the name as the first new hire in Ethiopia this year.

"Yes, the new program director," Almaz said.

Her words startled Ella, as Melody was listed on payroll as the Ethiopia HR manager. "Almaz," Ella said, her voice sharp as she started considering possibilities. "As far as I knew, *you* were the program director."

"Perhaps you were not aware," Almaz said softly. "Melody Lyles was brought on as program director six months ago. She presides over all three sites, and each has its own manager. I manage the Addis site only now."

Ella sensed hurt in Almaz's tone and she couldn't blame her. She had been the heartbeat of the overseas program since its inception. Why not hire a new manager for the Addis site and preserve Almaz's role as program director?

"Do you have her contact information?" Ella asked.

"Yes, sure," the woman said, reaching for her cell phone. She scrolled down and offered to forward the contact information to Ella.

"Thank you," Ella said. "I'll call her as soon as we leave. We'll get this sorted out."

"Yes, okay," Almaz said, her smile returning. "Please, have a lovely day." She leaned over to Bereket to tell him where to take them for supplies and then waved as the van drove away.

Ella was already pulling her phone out and dialing the number Almaz had given, her pulse roaring in her ears. With nearly two million funneling to Ethiopia in the past nine months, the Addis program should be thriving, not scaling back. It was certainly thriving on paper and in the bank account. Hopefully the mysterious Melody Lyles would have answers that made sense.

The call went straight to voice mail and Ella sighed, ending the connection.

"Voice mail?" Roman asked.

"Yes." She frowned. "What Almaz said really has me really worried."

"If anything, the programs here should be flourishing," Roman agreed.

"And what about the money raised from church this weekend? She didn't say anything about it, now that I think of it."

"We'll ask her when we go back to the site later," Roman said.

Ella's phone rang and she answered it, assuming Melody was calling her back. Instead, it was Patty Wright.

"Hi, Ella," she said urgently. "I'm so glad I got through to you."

Ella's heart lurched, immediately worried about her mother. "Is everything okay?"

"No," Patty answered, her voice cracking. "Hank has been arrested."

Ella was at once relieved that the bad news didn't involve her mom and shocked to hear the pastor had been arrested. "Oh, no, Patty. What happened?"

"He's being charged with…" Her voice caught. "Marilynn's murder."

"What? No…" The pastor a murderer? The idea didn't ring true. Then again, if he had actually been having an affair with Marilynn…

"JT called in a tip about that necklace Hank gave me for our anniversary," Patty continued, her words rushing together. "Turns out, it was Marilynn's. The police think…" She cleared her throat. "The police think he's been leading a double life."

Ella reached for an appropriate response as Patty finally stopped talking and broke down on the other end of the line. "This is unbelievable," Ella finally offered. "I'm so sorry, Patty. Is there anything I can do for you?"

"I'm hoping you can get Doug to call me back."

"Doug?" Ella asked, confused since she rarely spent much time with Patty's son. "I haven't spoken with him since Sunday. You may not have heard that I'm in Ethiopia right now and—"

"I know. That's why I'm calling you. He took the flight after yours. When you see him, can you make sure he calls me?"

"I will," Ella promised, wondering why Doug had decided to fly out, but figuring this wasn't the time for questions. "Anything else I can do?"

"No, Ella. Thank you, though."

"Take care, okay? I'll be in touch later," Ella assured her.

They said goodbye and Ella met Roman's questioning look.

She filled him in on what Patty had told her, and he just shook his head.

"Things keep getting stranger and stranger," he said as they piled out of the van to purchase the supplies for Graceway. "Wonder why Doug decided to fly out here early."

"Maybe he'll be on site when we get back and we can ask him," Ella said, but she was too preoccupied with the pastor's arrest and the mysterious Melody Lyles to worry about Doug.

It took much longer to secure the supplies than Roman had anticipated. It wasn't nearly as simple as a trip to Walmart would have been back home.

Nonetheless, they were able to get the supplies back to Graceway a little after three. Doug had come and gone by then, not responding to Ella's phone calls, but assuring her via text that he would call his mother. He also let her know that he had gone to the Graceway village south of town to speak with the community members about the delay in opening, and he invited Ella to catch up with him there. So, after dropping off the supplies, they all piled back into the van to head to the other site.

Mud huts dotted the landscape, the sun dipping a little lower by the minute as the van bumped along, the road disappearing and winding down into a grove of trees.

Bereket pulled over. "I will wait here," he said. "The van will not make it."

"How much farther?" Roman asked, opening the door and stepping out into tall grass.

"About a mile," Bereket said, examining the directions jotted in Amharic on a wrinkled sheet of notebook paper. "Follow this path right to the site."

"Okay, let's go," Roman said as Ella fell into step beside him.

"I'll jog up ahead and scout it out," Luke said. He took off at a quick jog, and Roman kept his attention on their surroundings, feeling a little uneasy. This was the exact type of situation he had wanted to avoid—and why he could have used a bigger team. Uncontrolled environments were where most mistakes happened in his line of work.

"Wonder how they've gotten vehicles down here to build," Ella said, her sandals slipping over a pile of rocks. He grabbed her arm to steady her and they continued on their way, the only sound around them the swish of trees in the breeze and the crunch of their feet along the path.

Dusk approached, the cacophony of insects loud around them, and somewhat mesmerizing. And something about the way the sunset played on Ella's hair, her cheeks rosy from exertion and humidity, made Roman want to reach over and take her hand. But this wasn't a romantic walk at the end of a lighthearted date, and too much had come between them to ever truly repair.

Still, there was something he'd never said to her that he'd been needing to say for years.

The timing didn't feel right, but then, when would it be? The best timing would have been six years ago. The more time that passed, the harder the words became.

"You know, Ell, I've always had one regret," he said, the words slipping out as they followed the rough path.

He cleared his throat against the unexpected emotions that welled up. "After Brooklyn died—"

"Roman, don't." Ella cut him off, her voice quiet and sad.

"Don't what?" he asked.

"Have regrets," she said. "We were different

people then," she added. "No one could have prepared us for what happened."

"True, but there's no way around this one regret," he said. "That one night, remember it?
You'd called me, crying."

She nodded.

"You said you couldn't stop thinking about
how if you hadn't suggested the movie, Brooklyn would still be alive."

She met his eyes for a moment, tears shimmering there. "It was true," she said, her voice breaking right along with his heart.

He stopped and turned to her.

"It wasn't," he insisted. "Maybe she would
have still been alive for another hour, another
day, another week. But there was no stopping
him. I should have told you that."

She shook her head. "You didn't want to go
to the movie. I pressed you," she said, her gaze
dropping to her hands. "Nothing you can say can
change that."

"In my grief, in that moment, I let you take the
blame," he admitted. "It was easier than taking it
all myself. But I felt just as much guilt—if I had
stayed close to campus, if I had insisted we stay.
I didn't want to face those feelings. I need you to
know that it wasn't your fault, and I never truly
thought it was."

He gently nudged her chin up so he could meet

her eyes again. "If I could go back and change that conversation, I would," he said. "I'm sorry."

In her eyes, he saw all that could have been. Maybe, if they had mourned differently. Maybe, if their grief hadn't torn them apart. And, for a brief moment, he thought that maybe there was hope for their future.

But Ella's expression was drawn and reserved, sheer agony in her eyes. Where he thought his apology would soothe any regrets she may hold on to, it seemed to have only brought up the sharp sting of the past.

"It was my fault, Roman," she said with conviction.

He took her hand in his. "No, it—"

"There's something I never told you."

The tone of her voice sent ice through his veins and he released her fingers from his grasp, waiting with dread for what she was about to say.

"I knew about the canceled classes. Brooklyn texted me and asked for us to come meet her. She thought I was in the library. I told her we were at the movies and suggested she find someone else."

She paused, as if giving him time for her words to sink in. "That's why she decided to go with a friend. I told her we were at the movies. If I had just said yes…if I had just told you then…" Her voice trailed off and Roman's gut clenched as he thought back to that night and recalled in vivid detail what had happened.

"I waited until she'd found someone to walk with her before I told you," Ella continued, silent tears streaming down her cheeks. She wiped them away, but more followed. "I didn't really think she was in danger. I thought your family was being overprotective. I—"

"Roman!" Luke's shout from up ahead caught both their attention. He had reappeared and was jogging back in their direction, his pace quick. Roman knew from the look in Luke's eyes that something was wrong.

"What's going on?"

"There's nothing there!"

Ella frowned, wiping her face quickly and recovering from the conversation neither of them had wanted to have.

Roman had so much more he needed to say to Ella, to ask her. But there wasn't time.

"What do you mean?" Ella asked, her voice thick. She cleared her throat.

Luke motioned for them to follow. "Come on, it's just around the corner."

SIXTEEN

Roman and Ella caught up with Luke and, sure enough, when they rounded the corner, where a large residential facility should be in the last stages of construction, there was what appeared to be the shabby beginnings of a concrete foundation in the middle of an otherwise empty field.

"There's supposed to be a compound of three large buildings here," Ella said. "The last report stated that we were a month away from opening the doors."

"Where's Doug?" Roman asked, warily watching the surrounding copse of trees.

"And why would he ask us to meet him here to tour *this*?" Ella pointed out. "Are we in the right place? Maybe they started construction here but changed the site location."

"I don't know, but I don't like the feel of this," Roman responded.

"Me neither," Luke said from across the clearing where he'd been scanning the perimeter. "If we turn around now, we should be able to make it back before it's too dark."

"I'll give Doug a call on the way to the van," Roman said.

Ella snapped a few photos of the barren site and the trio started back down the path.

Roman put a call in to Doug, but it went to voice mail and he pocketed his phone. "No answer," he said. "If this *was* the right place, I guess we know where the money has *not* been going."

Roman was on edge and he could tell Luke was, too. Where was Doug? Why wasn't he answering the phone? And why was there so little completed on the site's construction?

Their steps were hurried as they covered the distance back down the path, and Roman kept his attention vigilantly on their surroundings. Around them, though, the trees were still, night descending quickly.

Every minute ticked by with added tension as the three made their way to the van.

Roman spotted the last curve in the road ahead, knew they were close to the van—which meant they were close to safety. He hoped this was all a strange misunderstanding but—

A honking noise blared from up ahead and Roman's adrenaline kicked into overdrive. Someone was laying on a car horn.

"What on earth?" Ella said.

"We need to get back to Bereket," Luke said.

He glanced at Ella's sandaled feet. "I'll run ahead," he offered, taking off at a fast clip.

"I can run," Ella said. She started off after Luke, holding her own, despite her impractical footwear.

They were miles from everything except for remote villages where few people owned cars, and they had only seen a handful of vehicles during the last half hour of their trip. There was no doubt in Roman's mind that the honking was coming from Bereket's van. But why? Was he trying to hurry them along because night was coming? Wouldn't he have just called them? Or was he trying to warn them?

The honking suddenly stopped and the trees around them fell eerily silent as they raced along the path. Luke had gotten far enough ahead that they couldn't see him any longer.

Roman hoped they were running for no reason, and had almost convinced himself that the sound had come from another random passing car. But then, *crack!* A gunshot split the air and Ella gasped as he yanked her off the path and into the thick of the trees. The blast echoed, birds escaping the foliage overhead.

Ella looked at him, eyes wide with fear.

He held a finger to his lips and led her deeper, away from the path. He could make out the clearing ahead, knew they were close to the van. There was no sign of Luke, and Roman prayed the shot hadn't been aimed at him.

He motioned to a mass of overgrown shrubs and Ella crouched down behind them.

Positioning himself behind the trunk of a tree, he peered through the foliage to the van. He couldn't see Bereket, or Luke, for that matter. Was this some sort of a trap? It reeked of one.

He searched the surrounding trees, ensuring that it was a good place for Ella to take cover. "Stay right here," he whispered and then darted away from the hiding place.

He didn't want to leave her there, but he couldn't risk bringing her out in the open. He crouched low, hurrying toward the van, nerves on high alert. He had every disadvantage: he didn't know the terrain, he didn't have a weapon, and he didn't have any backup. It was enough to shake his confidence, but he'd spent years learning to work with what he had.

He reached the van and skirted around to the driver's side, but then stopped short. He took in the scene all at once. Bereket in the driver's seat, passed out, his head lolled to one side, his hands duct-taped securely behind his back. Luke, crumpled on the ground, blood pooling underneath him.

Roman took one last glance around, seeing no one. But he knew someone was there, someone who was likely expecting Ella next. He needed to get back to her, but he couldn't leave Luke bleeding like this. If he did, he wouldn't have a chance. Quickly, he turned his longtime friend onto his back and discovered the source of the blood—a bullet wound to his right thigh.

Roman yanked off his polo and shredded it down the seams, fashioning it into a tourniquet and tying it tightly around Luke's thigh. Luke moaned, his eyes blinking opened.

"Hang tight," Roman told him. "I'm getting you out of here."

He hoped he'd be able to. Luke's ashen face told him they didn't have much time to spare. He needed to get Luke in the van, move Bereket and then try to get Ella safely to the van.

Pulling out his phone and dialing to reach Addis police, he opened the back door to transfer Luke.

Someone answered speaking Amharic, and Roman opened his mouth to request an English speaker when Ella's scream rent the air.

He put the phone on Luke's chest. "Talk to them," he said urgently.

Hoping his friend would be able to, he popped up from behind the van, his attention lighting on Ella's hiding spot.

She was there, frozen. Doug Wright was behind her, holding her captive and pressing a gun to her temple.

"This is what we're gonna do, DeHart!" Doug

yelled out. "I've got a plane to catch in three hours, and you two aren't going to get in my way."

Doug's eyes were bright, his hair mussed, his demeanor manic and dangerous.

"*Someone* froze Graceway's assets, and turns out Ella here is the only one who can help me withdraw my pay. So, she's coming with me. You're staying here. Your friends are in tough shape, and no one's going to find you here for a long time. If she's a good girl, she can call for help once she gets me what I need.

"If she tries anything, well… I don't think there's a lot of hope for you out here. Now, I want the car keys and all the cell phones."

"Put the gun down, Doug," Roman said, not moving an inch. "You won't get away with this. You'll wind up right back in jail."

Doug stared back coldly and cocked the gun. "Now," he said.

Roman backed away, keeping his eyes on the pair as he hurried to the van, his mind reaching for a solution. He needed to get that gun—and Ella—away from Doug.

He found the keys and gathered the phones, jogging back toward Doug with the items.

"That's far enough!" Doug shouted, and Roman stopped.

"Toss them over here," Doug said.

Roman did as he was asked, his eyes seeking Ella's, silently telling her he was going to take care of her. The fear in her eyes only strengthened his resolve.

"Good," Doug said. "But I don't trust him," he said to Ella, suddenly aiming his gun straight at Roman.

"Kill him, and you won't get a cent," Ella quickly warned.

Doug hesitated for the barest moment and then reached into a pocket and handed Ella a roll of duct tape. "Tape up his wrists and ankles."

Ella stood frozen, the duct tape in her hands.

"Do it!" Doug yelled, and Ella jumped, taking a step toward Roman.

Roman held out his wrists, calculating. The closer she was, the easier this would be. It would be risky, but nothing was as risky as letting Ella go off in a car with this nut.

"It's okay, Ella," Roman said quietly.

She tried to lift the edge of the tape, but her hands were trembling and she couldn't catch the grip.

"You open it," Doug ordered, and Roman took the tape from her hands. "If you had just listened to my suggestion and stayed home, Ella, none of this would have had to happen." Doug's voice dripped with hatred.

"None of this has to happen at all," Roman said. "You can still turn back and do the right thing."

Doug laughed, the sound harsh and humorless. "Hurry up," he growled.

Roman could read the frenzy in Doug's eyes, the panic setting in as he realized whatever plan he had set out to accomplish was in real danger.

Roman knew he would only get one chance. He prayed it would be enough.

He grabbed the edge of the duct tape and tore a long starter piece to mask his voice as he whispered into Ella's ear, "Drop to the ground on three, two, *one.*"

She dropped right on cue and rolled sideways as Roman dove forward, low to the ground, and slammed his body weight into Doug's legs, sending him backward. The gun went off, blasting into the air and hitting trees behind them. Doug lowered his arm, but before he could even attempt to aim, Roman grabbed his wrist and wrenched it back, bones cracking as Doug howled in pain and dropped the weapon to the dusty ground.

Roman didn't give him a chance to recover; he slammed a fist into his nose, momentarily stunning him, and grabbed the gun off the ground. He swung downward, heavy steel connecting with the side of Doug's skull and knocking him out in one strike.

He turned to grab the duct tape, and Ella was already at his side, handing him the roll.

He wanted to pull her into his arms, to assure himself she was really alive, but they didn't have time to waste. They needed to get help for Bereket and Luke, and fast.

He handed her the two phones. "Try to call for help, and check Luke," he said to Ella.

As he secured Doug's wrists and ankles, sirens blared in the distance, lights flickering in the sky.

Doug started to regain consciousness, moaning in pain.

"I can't go back to jail," he wailed, his eyes pleading. "I can't."

Roman ignored him and jogged back to the van.

Ella was leaning over Luke, helping him sip water from a bottle from the cooler. Bereket had come to and was speaking rapid-fire Amharic into his cell phone.

As the police descended on the scene, Roman closed his eyes briefly, sending up a prayer of thanks for protection. Tonight could have gone another way in a heartbeat. He'd been given another chance and he vowed he wouldn't let it slip through his fingers.

SEVENTEEN

"It's on!" Triss announced from the living room, and Ella followed her mother from the kitchen to join the group that had gathered to watch the evening news. They'd spent the past two days steeped in the initial investigation, and the truth had all unfolded, but curiosity compelled them to watch the news segment regardless.

Roman and his crew had been busy dismantling the high-tech security system they'd installed, but they all set down tools and took seats around the room.

"Pastor Hank Wright of Anchor of Hope Fellowship in Annapolis has been released from jail, and his twenty-seven-year-old son, Doug Wright, sent back behind bars only a brief fourteen months after serving five years for armed robbery and assault of a police officer. Christy Spencer is standing just outside the Maryland Penitentiary now with the full story."

"And what a story it is," the newscaster said

into her microphone. "In a twisted tale between a pastor and his son, Doug Wright feigned his repentance and a changed life—it seems—all in the name of greed and revenge.

"Following nearly a decade of drug addiction and crime, Doug Wright claimed to have found the Lord, and was ready to change his ways. His book, *The Prodigal Son Returns*, written under the pen name Blake D. Wyatt, documents the trumped-up tale. His father accepted him into the fold, playing right into Doug's hands as he secretly siphoned funds from the church and the nonprofit it worked hand in hand with—Graceway. And, if that wasn't enough, he set into motion a series of tricks that would paint his minister father as a philandering murderer who had several affairs and took the life of local philanthropist, Marilynn Rice. We'll have more on this story tonight at ten."

"What a greedy psychopath," Triss muttered.

"Smart guy in some ways," Luke said from the recliner, where his bandaged leg was elevated on several pillows, still healing from the emergency surgery he'd received overseas. "He wove a complicated web."

"Took a lot of planning," Roman agreed, standing and excusing himself to finish up his work outside. His crew followed him, with the exception of Luke.

"I still can't believe he fooled me so easily," Ella's mom said. "And Wes, too."

"The accountant?" Luke asked.

Ella's mom nodded. "When the pastor offered Jim the open position at Graceway, Doug's friend was here at just the right time. I should have known it was suspicious."

"You couldn't have, Mom," Ella assured her. "Doug is a pathological liar and a master of deceit. He was the one who suggested his dad hire Jim in the first place. Even his own dad played right into his hands. It was the perfect setup for Doug to get access to Graceway—setting up a friend right in the financial heart of the company."

"But if I had just paid more attention," her mother continued. "All I needed to do was run a background check and I would have seen he had a record. Then, maybe Marilynn…"

Her eyes filled with tears and Triss lowered the volume on the TV, slipping out of the room as Roman's team quietly went back to their jobs.

"No one would have done anything differently," Ella said, "especially in the midst of running a business and dealing with cancer treatments." But she ached, knowing too well the guilt her mom would harbor for the rest of her life.

"I know you're right, honey, but I'll always wish that I had," her mom said, wiping away tears and reaching for a tissue on the coffee table.

Doug had been darkly clever and charmingly manipulative—even managing to sweet-talk the church secretary, Lacey, into his schemes.

Lacey Sage, aka Melody Lyles, had traveled to Ethiopia along with Doug and the tens of thousands she had saved that Graceway had been paying her for a job that didn't exist.

She had been the lying voice calling media and touting a romance with the pastor. She and Doug had been set to fly out of the country with the money at the end of the week when Doug had been scheduled for one of his quarterly mission trips. They'd planned to leave with the more than two million dollars Doug had managed to sock away in the Ethiopian account—with which Doug would continue to live the high life as an accomplished drug dealer. Unfortunately for them both, the frozen assets had inconveniently gotten in their way.

As had the discovery of Ella's fentanyl-laced Prozac, which had been contributing to her bouts of confusion and amnesia. A search warrant of Doug's apartment had yielded plenty of drug paraphernalia to point the finger at him for tampering with Ella's medicine. Having taken care of Isaac countless times, he may have had easy access to the house when Ella was working at Graceway. Whatever the case, now that Ella was on a fresh prescription, her memories had begun to return, her nausea and amnesia slowly subsiding.

"What do you think about Wes's story?" Triss asked, rolling her eyes.

"I don't buy it," Ella said, and her mother agreed.

Wes Bentley, who had been collecting the salaries of five fictional Graceway employees in exchange for his criminal help, had turned himself in and been charged with the third degree murder of Marilynn Rice.

Doug had tasked him with stealing the car and something valuable they could use to frame the pastor later. Wes claimed that he had waited until he'd thought Marilynn was gone and then entered through the back door, walking up the stairs to her bedroom.

But she'd still been at home, getting ready for her doctor's appointment. As he'd turned right on the landing, she'd raced out of a bedroom down the hall and run for the stairs. That's when she'd fallen. She'd died without a hand ever touching her. His claimed remorse was suspicious, considering he'd had the presence of mind to remove the woman's necklace after her fall. The necklace Doug had taken and given to his father, claiming he'd seen it online and just knew it would be perfect for his dad to give his mother for their anniversary.

The whole sordid affair was impossible to understand. It was the workings of a madman. And, even though there was no proof yet, Ella was certain he was responsible for her mom's accident.

Along with the slow return of her memories, Ella could now vividly recall waking to Doug's face near hers, his gloved hand encompassing hers before that first shot went off weeks ago. He must have known people would get suspicious after her mom's accident and Marilynn's death. He'd tried to use what he'd known about Ella—and what he'd learned from his handful of dates with Autumn—to his advantage. But when the suicide-murder attempts kept failing, he'd realized time was running out.

"Do you really have to leave tonight, honey?" Ella's mom asked, pulling her from her thoughts.

"My flight leaves at nine," she said. "I've stayed about as long as I can."

"What will you do now?" her mom asked, her gaze sliding over to where Roman had just pulled a surveillance cam from outside the front windows.

"The same old thing," Ella said, ignoring her mother's pointed look. Her heart had already withdrawn itself from Roman. They'd both been busy since they'd gotten back to the States, and they both knew she'd be going home soon. Her coming back here, the feelings that had rekindled—none of that changed the past and what Ella had done, unintentional or not.

Her mom was watching her thoughtfully. "I just want you to be happy, Ella."

"I'm happy, Mom," Ella said. "And I'll visit more often, too. Maybe go on a trip or two with you."

"I'd like that. But…"

"But what?"

"Don't you ever get lonely?"

Ella laughed. "Mom, you raised all of us on your own, and showed us how fulfilling life could be, married or not."

Her mom's gaze softened, her eyes just a little sad. "It was lonely at times, Ella, I won't lie. I want more for you."

Ella's heart pitched at her mother's admission, but there was no going back now. Her flight was set and her clinic was expecting her first thing in the morning.

"I'm happy, Mom," she repeated. "Come visit me and see for yourself. Once JT gets more established at the helm of Graceway, you'll have some time on your hands."

"I'll definitely be visiting you, sweetie," her mom said.

Ella had mixed feelings when her mother told her that JT would be taking the reins at Graceway. The organization had been her mother's life and Ella worried that she may start to feel irrelevant if she wasn't leading. But her mom seemed at peace and relieved by the change in leadership and there was no denying JT's exuberance and passion for the program.

Interesting, she thought suddenly, how something so perfect could come from such an awful crime. Had prayers effected that outcome, or had God simply chosen to make something beautiful out of something devastating? There were all those pesky questions again—questions that begged for answers. But the only answer Ella kept coming to was the idea of surrender her mother had talked about.

For the first time in years, she was beginning to feel a sense of peace again, despite all the tragedy she had experienced. Or, maybe, in a way, because of it.

One thing was certain: Doug Wright's crimes were finally exposed to the light. And from the darkest of greed and lack of humanity came a public outpouring of love and support for Graceway. So, in turn, hundreds and eventually thousands more families would be taken care of.

Ella's heart was full, faith rooting itself deeply in her soul. She had never been alone. Even in the darkest moments, she'd had a silent witness. One who carried her even when she had fooled herself into believing she was walking on her own two feet.

"Well, let me get my keys and coat," her mother said, apparently giving up on the idea that Ella would change her flight. "We'll head out in a few minutes…if you want to say goodbye to anyone."

Roman had finished attaching a new rain gutter and was stepping down off the ladder to reach for something in the toolbox when Ella walked outside.

"Hey," she said, willing her voice to be casual as she approached across the crisp lawn, drawing her scarf tighter around her neck.

He straightened, his gaze floating over her face and touching on her suitcase.

"Thought your fight didn't leave until nine tomorrow?" he said, stepping closer.

Ella memorized the soft curve of his lips, the strong angle of his jaw, the cold-induced pink on his cheeks that made him look younger and almost convinced her they had never missed a heartbeat.

"No, nine tonight," she clarified.

Her gaze caught on the fresh coat of paint he'd applied to the shutters, and the wheelbarrow full of mulch his team was busy dispersing to clean up her mom's garden beds. "I wanted to thank you for everything, Roman. I—"

He held up a hand. "No thanks necessary. I'm just glad we all came through it in one piece."

She smiled. "That makes two of us," she said with a soft laugh. "You're really good at what you do, you know that?"

"You're a pretty good partner," he said, and her heart skipped a beat. "Aside from the disappearing act and all," he added, and she laughed out loud that time, his humor contagious.

"Just keeping you on your toes," she teased. She rocked back on her heels and crossed her arms over her chest. "Anyway," she said, fighting a growing lump in her throat. "I'm glad we got to catch up, even if the circumstances weren't ideal."

She opened her arms to him and he wrapped her in his embrace. Ella hung on just a moment longer than she probably should have, breathing in his scent one last time. It was somehow harder to walk away this time than it had been years ago.

"Stay," he whispered in her ear, so quietly Ella wasn't sure she hadn't imagined it.

She pulled back, meeting his eyes.

"All those things you told me, back in Ethiopia…about that night. I knew already," he said.

Her heart dropped.

"What?"

"During the trial," he explained. "Brooklyn's text records were pulled up."

"You never told me…"

"I never blamed you, Ella," he said. "I might have done the same thing if she'd texted me, I don't know. You didn't cause her death. Jason Branson is at fault. Not you."

She shook her head, even as new hope thrummed in her veins. "But you let me leave that summer," she said. "And…when Shield opened—" She stopped herself.

"What?" he prodded.

"I came that day," she admitted. "To the grand opening. I wasn't going to, but I couldn't stay away." She watched him as understanding dawned in his eyes.

"You saw Shannon," he said quietly. "After I got your note and realized you weren't coming, my brother set me up on a blind date." He grinned. "He said he was tired of watching me mope around."

Roman stroked a teardrop from Ella's cheek, but another one took its place. "It didn't go anywhere," he said. "It couldn't. Not when I was still in love with you."

Ella's heart constricted at his confession.

"Stay here," he said, his eyes intent on hers. "Marry me."

Her breath caught in her throat. "It's not that simple," she whispered.

"Sure it is," he said, capturing her mouth in a tender kiss.

But he pulled back just an inch, his eyes searching hers. "If you don't want to stay, I'll come to you."

"What? Pack up everything and just relocate? You can't, Roman. You've spent years building Shield and—"

"I don't want to spend another day of my life

without you," he said, cutting off her protest. "I loved you when we were teenagers and I love you more today."

She could hardly catch her breath with the knowledge he would give up everything just to start a life with her. Of course, she wouldn't ask him to. The truth was she missed her hometown, and she had two veterinarians working for her who would love to purchase the practice so she could relocate.

"It's very simple. One word and our lives change today."

Her heart burst into a million happy pieces and she kissed him again and then grinned. She did always make things more complicated than they needed to be. "Yes," she said, her heart dancing. "Is that the word you were looking for?"

He laughed and pulled her close. "I wouldn't mind hearing it again," he whispered in her ear.

"I've loved you for as long as I can remember," she whispered back, her heart in her throat. "So, yes," she repeated, looking into his eyes and imagining their future unfolding together the way she'd always dreamed it would. "Yes, to forever."

* * * * *

*If you liked this story from Sara K. Parker,
check out her first book:*

UNDERCURRENT

Available now from Love Inspired Suspense!

Find more great reads at
www.LoveInspired.com

Dear Reader,

On a breezy, sunny November day, I took my feverish nine-year-old daughter to the doctor to rule out strep or the flu. Turned out, she had cancer. For weeks, I cried every time I surfaced from sleep, repeatedly whispering one tiny prayer. Please, let her live.

And He did! As I write this letter, Aaliyah is one week away from completing ten months of treatment for Ewing's Sarcoma, her tumor has been one hundred percent eradicated, and she and her twin sister can't wait to start fifth grade.

As I watch our daughter overcome terrible odds and start to reclaim her childhood, my heart bursts with gratefulness, but also grieves for other cancer families I've met along the way. Cancer's indiscriminate nature stirs up questions with no tidy answers—questions about faith, prayer, suffering and surrender.

In *Dying to Remember*, Ella Camden wrestles with her faith and the purpose of prayer after a personal tragedy evokes questions she can't find satisfying answers to. But when a deadly threat reunites her with childhood sweetheart Roman DeHart, Ella begins to discover a sense of peace in the steady, unfailing presence of God.

In a world that sometimes blindsides us with heartbreak, my prayer is that you experience that peace, too, clinging to God as your anchor—no matter what the future holds. Drop me a line through my web site at www.sarakparker.com. I'd love to hear from you.

With love,
Sara K. Parker

Get 4 FREE REWARDS!

We'll send you 2 FREE Books
plus 2 FREE Mystery Gifts.

Love Inspired® books feature contemporary inspirational romances with Christian characters facing the challenges of life and love.

FREE
Value Over
$20

Get 4 FREE REWARDS!

We'll send you 2 FREE Books plus 2 FREE Mystery Gifts.

Harlequin® Heartwarming™ Larger-Print books feature traditional values of home, family, community and most of all—love.

FREE
Value Over
$20

YES! Please send me 2 FREE Harlequin® Heartwarming™ Larger-Print novels and my 2 FREE mystery gifts (gifts worth about $10 retail). After receiving them, if I don't wish to receive any more books, I can return the shipping statement marked "cancel." If I don't cancel, I will receive 4 brand-new larger-print novels every month and be billed just $5.49 per book in the U.S. or $6.24 per book in Canada. That's a savings of at least 19% off the cover price. It's quite a bargain! Shipping and handling is just 50¢ per book in the U.S. and 75¢ per book in Canada*. I understand that accepting the 2 free books and gifts places me under no obligation to buy anything. I can always return a shipment and cancel at any time. The free books and gifts are mine to keep no matter what I decide.

161/361 IDN GMY3

Name (please print)

Address   Apt. #

City   State/Province   Zip/Postal Code

Mail to the **Reader Service:**
IN U.S.A.: P.O. Box 1341, Buffalo, NY 14240-8531
IN CANADA: P.O. Box 603, Fort Erie, Ontario L2A 5X3

Want to try two free books from another series! Call 1-800-873-8635 or visit www.ReaderService.com.

HOME *on the* RANCH

HRCBPA18